"How do you [...] so much ab[...]"

Zana studied Brian then added, "It sounds as if you had me investigated."

"Not you. Your father." Brian looked at her with animosity. "I won't have my mother's heart broken by some conniving bridegroom. Have I made myself clear?"

"Quite," Zana said stiffly. "What's clear is that without knowing my father—without even *meeting* him—you've judged him...not at all favorably."

"I don't have to meet him to know plenty. I just hope he realizes he can't have everything he wants."

"What are you talking about?"

"I'm talking about Zachary House. Obviously he thinks he can get back his ancestral home simply by marrying my mother. But the price is higher than that. He's made his choice, now he'd better pretend to be the happiest, most in-love man around. Or else..."

Kate Denton is a pseudonym for the Texas writing team of Carolyn Hake and Jeanie Lambright. Friends as well as coauthors, they concur for the most part on politics and good Mexican restaurants, but disagree about men—tall versus short—and what constitutes good weather—sun versus showers. One thing they do agree on, though, is the belief that romance is not just for the young!

Books by Kate Denton

NO OBJECTIONS
Kate Denton

𝓗𝓪𝓻𝓵𝓮𝓺𝓾𝓲𝓷 𝓑𝓸𝓸𝓴𝓼

TORONTO • NEW YORK • LONDON
AMSTERDAM • PARIS • SYDNEY • HAMBURG
STOCKHOLM • ATHENS • TOKYO • MILAN
MADRID • WARSAW • BUDAPEST • AUCKLAND

To the "other" Zana, with many thanks for your support and encouragement

ISBN 0-373-03281-1

Harlequin Romance first edition September 1993

NO OBJECTIONS

CHAPTER ONE

"YOU'RE MARRIED?"

Zana sat gripping the telephone, unable to believe what she was hearing. Occasionally a few muffled words penetrated her consciousness.

"Of course, Caroline's younger.... She's as cute as a button.... You're going to love her as much as I do...."

After long moments Zana came out of her daze, but instead of her father's voice, she heard only the dial tone. She returned the receiver to its cradle, then dropped her head into her hands.

"What's he gotten himself into now?" she moaned aloud. Every time she relaxed her guard, Russell Zachary managed to end up in trouble. It had been that way for years—in fact, all her life. One would almost think she was the parent and he the child. She began to wonder if she should have gone by the house to check on him, instead of driving straight to her ballet studio. But then she realized that would have been fruitless, since Russell wasn't *at* home.

"This isn't getting me anywhere," she decided, straightening her spine. It wouldn't do any good to become frenzied. Her father wasn't about to change. Men approaching seventy rarely did.

But *marriage!* He'd given no clue, not even the slightest hint, that he was planning this. What could have happened during those few days she was away in Jackson? Zana opened her appointment calendar to June and tried to recount the events of the past week. *Let's see... Papa and I went to a concert on Thursday night, then Friday I left for the weekend sessions of the ballet competition....*

On Friday evening, she'd spoken to him by telephone, then again on Saturday, and early today—Monday—she'd returned to Natchez. No mention had been made of any Caroline during that time. And before that? Zana frowned. She was positive she'd never heard her father talk about Caroline, or any other woman for that matter, since they'd moved to Natchez.

Now, out of the blue, he was announcing that he'd gotten married. Without warning. Without anything. How could he do this to her—to the memory of her mother—and expect Zana to be pleased? Vivi Zachary had been dead less than a year. Had he recovered from the tragedy that soon? And where had he found his bride? When she'd asked, Russell had put her off, mumbling something about one of his walks. Zana suspected there was more to their meeting than a chance encounter during a morning stroll. She shook her head and sighed.

Her next class arrived within minutes of the fateful call, giving Zana insufficient time to compose herself. She was hardly able to pay attention to the steps she had to teach, but by rote she managed to get through the warm-up exercises with the children. Fortunately the little girls were too young to notice her detachment.

Zana was of medium height, about two feet taller than her charges, with a lithe dancer's body and skin so fair it looked translucent. Dressed as she was in a pink leotard and short georgette skirt, with matching pink tights covering her long shapely legs, she was the personification of the twirling figurine on the top of a music box.

Few people could guess the tights also covered the ugly scar that slashed across her left knee. Except for a tiny mark at the edge of her temple, all physical evidence of the accident was hidden. Still, the outer blemishes were minor compared to the scars that marked her soul.

As she watched the youngsters do their routines at the bar, Zana rested one hand on the back of a chair for support. Her knee hurt more than usual today. Stress, coupled with the weather, she told herself. The skies had been wrapped in an ominous gray when she'd arrived, but with a windowless studio, she had no way of knowing what was happening now. The ache in her knee said it was raining though. She'd be glad when this session was over, so that she could go home and prop her leg up until the pain subsided.

She limped over to the cassette player and fast-forwarded the tape. Tchaikovsky's "Waltz of the Flowers" began playing and she closed her eyes for a moment to listen. When she opened them, tears threatened to spill onto her cheeks. Tchaikovsky had been her mother's favorite composer; she'd loved to see Zana dance to his pieces. Now the music only served as a reminder of how much had changed.

Zana admonished herself for the show of weakness. Being unable to perform Tchaikovsky on stage was a small loss. There had been a much greater one—one her father had apparently put behind him. She felt a stab of resentment, not for the first time and undoubtedly not for the last. She loved him dearly, but Russell Zachary could be a most irritating man.

She returned her attention to the eight little girls, all under the age of six. They were standing in a row with their backs to the mirror, miniature versions of Zana in their leotards, tights and pink ballet shoes. But while Zana's silken waist-length hair was the color of midnight, the children's tresses were lighter and more subdued—baby blond, chestnut brown, soft red.

The lesson was almost over when she spied a man through the observation glass, pacing the floor of the reception area like an expectant father in a maternity ward. Who was he? Zana thought she'd met all her students' parents.

It must have been raining in earnest. A trio of moms sitting near the stranger clutched umbrellas, and even in the glare of the glass, she could tell the man's hair was damp and his suit jacket soaked with moisture. Zana pitied the child he'd come for, because he looked none too happy about being here today.

In fact, he looked absolutely furious, probably because his pride and joy hadn't been given a starring role in the recent recital, she thought. And probably ready to upbraid her about it. Teaching was rewarding, but it had its downside, too. *Just what I need after Papa's news—a confrontation with someone else's daddy.*

Whoever he was, he was attracting plenty of attention from the waiting mothers. Perhaps he wasn't a local father. Mindy's mother, Zana noticed, had abandoned her needlepoint to shamelessly size him up, and Sara's mom cupped a hand over her mouth as she whispered to Liza's mother. Natchez was not exactly a metropolis; most of the parents were friends or acquaintances, at least. The newcomer seemed to be a stranger to these three.

Zana turned her attention to the children. She could feel the man's eyes on her as she continued the ballet lesson. "Show me first position," she instructed her students. The children's arms rounded in ovals, and tiny sets of heels formed vees on the polished studio floor as she tried to concentrate on teaching and ignore her observer.

Calling for second position, she involuntarily looked through the glass and caught his gaze. He tapped a fingernail on his watch crystal, a clear sign for her to hurry up. Well, Mr. Impatient would just have to wait. This was her job, and she wouldn't abort a session simply because some autocratic male thought she should.

The remaining five minutes of the lesson seemed like an hour, then it took several more minutes for the mothers to exchange greetings and hustle their daughters away, all the while glancing speculatively at Zana's visitor.

She'd somehow expected him to charge into the studio the moment the class was over. Instead, with a shoulder propped against the wall, he lingered in the reception area, allowing the crowd to disperse.

Fifteen minutes had passed by the time the last mother and daughter had left. It was only then that he strode over to Zana. "Where are they?" His voice was low, but his manner was intimidating. He towered over her, his brow furrowed and his winged eyebrows as threatening as the devil incarnate. She could almost see the smoke billowing from his ears. But this was no dark and sinister Lucifer—her visitor had sandy-colored hair and vivid green eyes that had flashes of light flickering in their depths.

"*They?*" Zana was completely confused.

"Don't be coy, Miss Zachary," he said. "I want to know where your father has taken her."

Her? It took a moment for Zana to understand. The *her* was obviously Russell Zachary's new wife— and just as obviously, someone very important to the man before her.

Her body relaxed slightly. He was angry, but at least now she knew why. "As you can see, Mr...."

"Westbrook, Brian Westbrook."

She gestured around the empty room. "Neither of them is here, Mr. Westbrook. And I'm not exactly sure where they are." Needing to sit down, she moved to her office. Perhaps between the two of them, they could make some sense of what had happened.

He followed her, and positioned himself on the edge of the chair she indicated. "I suppose *you* were all for it," he said accusingly.

She stared at him, too surprised to form an immediate reply. She felt resentment build within her once more, both at her father and at the rude Brian Westbrook.

Zana prided herself on her ability to control her emotions. She'd had much experience dealing with temperamental partners and her demanding father, and had cultivated an ability to remain calm even when she felt ready to explode like an overinflated balloon. She'd always channeled her energies into ballet rather than wasting them on anger. But at the moment, she was tempted to throw something lethal at her unwanted visitor. Booting him out the door would have been satisfying, too.

"I thought so," he continued, apparently taking her silence for assent. "Well, since you were a co-conspirator, you must know where they are." His fingers agitatedly drummed on her desk.

"I was *not* part of any conspiracy!" Zana's last hold on her self-control snapped, and she rose to her feet to lean on the desk facing him. She'd had enough of this insolent intruder.

Who *was* Brian Westbrook? Was Papa's new wife his sister? Or perhaps, his ex-girlfriend? No, not a girlfriend, Zana decided. As charming as Russell Zachary could be, no sane young woman would choose him over the gorgeous male across from her. Even if the gorgeous male *had* displayed an appalling lack of manners.

"I think they're in New Orleans, so why don't you scurry down there and see if you can find them? Just keep me out of this!" She straightened to her full height, hands tightly clenched at her sides.

"Where in New Orleans?" he demanded.

"My father didn't say." She sighed. All the fight suddenly went out of her, leaving her terribly tired.

"And you wouldn't tell me if he had," he said.

It was as though he'd read her mind. Her distress at her father notwithstanding, Zana probably would have lied even if she was certain of the newlyweds' whereabouts. Her visitor looked angry enough to punch someone, and there was no doubt who would come out the loser in a confrontation between him and Russell Zachary.

He pointed an accusing finger at her. "Do you honestly think I'm going to let the two of you get away with this?"

"I'm telling you the truth!" Her voice was sharp, her indignation matching his. It *was* the truth— Russell hadn't told her where he was, although she suspected he and his bride might be at his sister Cil's. She brushed a loose strand of dark hair behind her ear. "Did it ever occur to you, Mr. Westbrook, that maybe I was upset, too? That only hours ago I learned about this marriage and now I have to contend with *you* barging into my life?"

He stared at her in surprise and, for the first time, actually seemed to see her. Faced with his intense gaze, Zana wished she'd taken a few moments to get dressed, instead of simply pulling off her short skirt. As often as she'd worn them, now she felt exposed in just tights and leotard.

Suddenly he shook his head as if trying to keep his mind on Caroline and her father. "I can see I'm getting nowhere with you." He reached into his breast pocket for a small case from which he pulled a business card. "Call me as soon as you hear anything," he commanded. Dropping the card on her desk, he left her office.

"Talk about gall," Zana muttered, dropping back into her chair. She sat silently, willing her pulse to steady before she picked up the card and tore it into tiny pieces. "That's what I think of your boorish behavior, Mr. Brian Westbrook," she said, throwing the pieces into a wastebasket. The Sahara would see snow before she called that obnoxious man.

ZANA TOOK her usual route home, not the most direct course, but the one she preferred, the one that passed by Zachary House, an antebellum mansion sitting proudly on a promontory overlooking the Mississippi River. All traces of rain had disappeared, replaced by a glaring midday sun that added luster to the mansion's fresh white paint.

When Zana and her father had returned to Natchez some months earlier, Zachary House had been like an aging, neglected dowager. It had remained that way until a few weeks ago. Now the dowager was getting a face-lift, with a trailer in the yard serving as headquarters for a construction crew working on the building.

The fence had already been repaired, effectively shutting out the curious from close exploration, but through the white wrought iron, Zana could see workmen on scaffolding. The new owners had to be well off, she thought. It must have taken a tidy sum to restore the battered weatherworn dwelling to its previous glory. But that was what was happening.

Zana lifted her foot from the brake and pressed the accelerator. She didn't have time to think about Zachary House today. She had more serious matters on her mind. Besides, a car was approaching, and she didn't want to be spotted inspecting the house that had once belonged to her family. It would embarrass her to be caught gawking at it like a small child at a candy store window.

Yet she was too intrigued with the renovations to ever consider another way home. Usually one glance at Zachary House was all it took to free her mind from any worries—even though it also brought her sadness. The house would have been hers, her inheritance, had her father not made that impossible.

Now home was a three-bedroom cottage on the outskirts of Natchez, neat, well kept and what Zana had become accustomed to. It was also undeniable proof of her family's lessened circumstances, especially when compared to the grandeur of Zachary House or their previous existence abroad.

For years the family had lived well, with Russell Zachary, a violinist, playing with several European orchestras. Her mother, Vivi, had been an accomplished harpist. The most talented of the Zacharys, however, was Zana. She'd been a soloist with the Royal Ballet by her eighteenth birthday, and she had since performed in all the major works—*Giselle, Swan Lake, Romeo and Juliet*. As artists, she and her parents had frequently been wined and dined, willing recipients of gracious hospitality. It was a lifestyle that all three had come to take for granted.

Then the accident changed everything. Zana's ballet career was halted abruptly and tragically, and only two of the family had returned to Natchez.

Zana wished she could control her thoughts and prevent the stabbing pain they generated. Today she was feeling something new—betrayal. How could her father forsake Vivi's memory by remarrying so quickly, and to a woman he hardly knew? He'd said his new wife was young. Younger than Vivi, who had been fifteen years his junior? Had he, a man with a history of making bad decisions, now fallen for someone no older than his daughter? The idea was ludicrous.

Zana didn't usually fret, but she couldn't help it now, despite telling herself that worrying was useless. What she really needed was more details. She'd call Aunt Cil. After all, the woman was a human information pipeline.

Zana juggled the telephone receiver while making a cup of herbal tea. She'd dialed several times in the past ten minutes and had gotten nothing except a busy signal. But that wasn't unusual. Aunt Cil spent a large part of each day with a receiver firmly attached to her ear and, since the invention of the cordless phone, had become almost impossible to reach.

Zana heard the cuckoo clock in the hall sound the hour. One o'clock. Still early. Forget about propping up the aching knee, she told herself. Just take a couple of aspirin, then hop in the car and drive to New Orleans. That would make more sense than spending hours repeatedly dialing the phone while her anxiety increased.

It was more than 150 miles, but the trip would be worth it if she could confront her father before Brian Westbrook got to him. Just the thought of that impossible man barging into her studio made Zana gnash her teeth.

She forced herself to stop thinking about him and concentrate on the trip instead. Since Aunt Cil, ever the Southern belle, hated seeing women in pants, Zana changed from her jeans into a khaki split skirt and replaced her tennis shoes with espadrilles. As an afterthought, she added hoop earrings that matched her red cotton blouse.

She wasn't hungry but, deciding she'd better eat something, quickly assembled a sandwich of cold chicken, lettuce and tomato and grabbed a can of diet soda to take along. She'd eat on the way.

Reaching New Orleans as soon as possible was her priority.

Zana drove almost automatically, her thoughts more on her father's latest escapade than on the scenery whizzing by. Usually she savored the beauty of the delta country, the tall pines flanking the roadside and the massive splendor of Lake Pontchartrain. But not today.

Until recently, Zana had been jittery about driving, especially on the highway. It had been only eleven months since the accident near Monte Carlo. The Zachary family had been taking a brief vacation when her mother, at the wheel, had swerved to avoid a goat on the road and lost control, flipping the car. She'd been killed instantly. Russell had managed to escape with bruises, but Zana, dozing in the back seat, had been trapped in the wreckage, her leg pinned by the twisted metal. She'd spent weeks in the hospital recovering from the injuries and trying to deal with the loss of her mother.

After Zana's release from the hospital, her disconsolate father had insisted on returning to his hometown. Consumed with despair, he seemed intent on joining his wife in death and, like many Americans from the Deep South, refused to die anywhere but Dixie.

Zana accompanied him to Mississippi. Having been informed by her doctors that her performing days were over, she had no reason to stay behind.

Besides, her heartsick father needed her. But the demise Russell Zachary hoped for didn't happen. He was morose for months, then the sadness had begun to ebb, and in the past few weeks Zana had seen glimpses of his old ebullience.

Even Zana's grief—for both her mother and her lost career—had started to ease. Then along came reality—money was short. The Zacharys' limited bank account and minimal life insurance had been depleted by Zana's medical bills. So she'd invested her remaining savings in a dance studio because ballet was all she knew.

It wasn't much, but at least she could keep a roof over their heads and take care of Russell, who hadn't picked up his violin since the accident, claiming he was too old and uninspired to renew his career.

Zana hadn't expected to enjoy teaching, but to her surprise found that she did. She couldn't deny she missed the thrill of performing, but introducing her young charges to the wonder of dance was fulfilling in its own way. Zana realized she was almost fully recovered emotionally when she accepted an invitation to attend the International Ballet Competitions and watch the promising new dancers. For her, agreeing to attend was a milestone.

The annual competitions were held in one of four locations throughout the world—Moscow; Helsinki; Varna, Bulgaria; and, somewhat improbably, Jackson, Mississippi. No one in Jackson seemed to think this was an unusual arrangement, though, and the residents were avid supporters.

While most Americans weren't aware of this gathering of ballet's elite, Zana had always been intrigued by the connection between her father's home state and the world of ballet. She'd even dreamed of some day participating as a guest soloist. A dream that, according to her doctors, would never come true.

Despite the physicians' prognoses that she wouldn't dance again, Zana was sure her leg was healing. Each day meant a little less discomfort and a little more control over movement. The damp weather did bring on a few aches, but compared to the agony she'd known, they were trivial.

The latest concern had been how she'd handle the trip into the past, forced to be a spectator without knowing how much of that life she could hope to regain.

Anticipating an emotional weekend, Zana had decided the best way to cope was to attend as many events as possible. She'd even agreed to return for the Awards Gala Performance next Saturday. Now this crazy marriage had upset her equilibrium once more.

Hours earlier she'd been patting herself on the back for accepting the challenge of facing the ballet world. It had taken only a phone call from Russell to plunge her into self-doubt. She tried not to be judgmental, but she was getting tired of her father's always putting himself first and giving no thought to how his actions would affect anyone else.

Her mental ramblings lasted the entire trip to New Orleans and, in what seemed like minutes, she found herself driving along the narrow streets of the French Quarter toward her aunt's town house.

Finding a parking space in front of a row of old black hitching posts, Zana walked the half block to Cil's. The French Quarter always lifted her spirits. For the most part, Zana's younger years had been spent at boarding schools in France and Spain, so she felt at home in New Orleans, with its European architecture and ambience. Even her slight European accent fit in here.

Russell Zachary and his two siblings, William and Lucille—Aunt Cil—had been brought up in the lap of luxury, thanks to the family business, the Zachary Trailer Company.

Even though he demonstrated absolutely no aptitude or interest in the business, it was understood that Russell, the eldest, would take over the company one day. Thus it came as a shock to the whole family when her father announced his intention to pursue a musical career in Europe, in effect turning his back on Zachary Trailers.

Uncle William, the younger son, had stepped in and gone into partnership with their father. But that wasn't enough to appease Grandfather Zachary. He never forgave Russell and sought revenge by leaving both the business and Zachary House to William.

Unfortunately Uncle William wasn't much of a businessman, either. By the time he died at fifty, a middle-aged bachelor, the company was in receivership, and Zachary House and its contents had been sold to pay debts.

Aunt Cil was actually the only one of the three with any head for business, but in those times a working woman was disapproved of, so she did the expected thing and married well. Happily, for the romantic Lucille, it was also a love match.

Soon after the wedding, Cil's bridegroom took her away to his family home in New Orleans where she enjoyed all the trappings of a rich man's wife until, sadly, she ended up a young widow. But thanks to the money bequeathed her by her late husband, she was able to maintain a comfortable existence in the New Orleans town house where Zana was now headed.

She'd just lifted the bronze lion's-head knocker on the front door when a voice sounded behind her.

"I *thought* you'd know where to find them."

Zana wheeled around, stunned to find Brian Westbrook on the step below her. "You followed me!"

"Yes, and it wasn't easy," he said. "You drive like a bat out of hell. I'm surprised we both aren't in jail right now."

Zana was shocked. She hadn't even realized she'd been driving over the speed limit. Normally she was a careful driver. Normally she never violated any laws. Especially since the accident. But this wasn't a normal day, and speeding was just another indication of how agitated she was about the marriage—and about Brian.

The door opened suddenly. "Zana, darling, what a pleasant surprise!" Aunt Cil wrapped her in an enthusiastic hug. "And who might this be?"

"Aunt Cil, this is Brian Westbrook. Mr. Westbrook, may I present Lucille Hebert." She pronounced it the way the French would, with a silent "h" and "t."

"Pleased to meet you," he said, his voice tinged with something that sounded less like pleasure and more like bemusement.

Aunt Cil had that effect on people. Today she was quite an eyeful, her turquoise-print caftan billowing around her in the breeze, her orange hair poufed about her head like a cloud of cotton candy and earrings the size of small saucers dangling from her ears. Her cheeks were rouged a lively pink, and purple shadow emphasized her sky-blue eyes. As always Aunt Cil looked like a color-mad fairy godmother.

"Well, come in, children, come in. I should have guessed you were Brian," Cil said, clutching his hand between her own in greeting. "Caroline said her son was handsome as all get out, and she wasn't exaggerating." She hugged him, too, then took each of her visitors by the elbow, escorting them down the hall.

Caroline's *son*. That made things a little clearer. Zana could now understand Brian's consternation at the marriage, having been every bit as put out as he, only not as aggressively vocal about it. Zana heaved a sigh of relief. This information eliminated one concern. If Caroline was Brian's mother, then her father's bride wasn't some twenty-year-old.

"I don't believe my eyes," Brian muttered as Aunt Cil led the way into the parlor, a room that, as far as eye-popping garishness went, complemented her perfectly. As Brian surveyed the surroundings, Aunt Cil gestured for them to have a seat, then perched on one of a pair of ivory damask-covered love seats. Zana sat on the other.

The room was crammed full of old-fashioned knickknacks, an abundance of paintings, including a Monet and an Andy Warhol hung side by side, Victorian lamps, an Oriental rug, overstuffed chairs and a multitude of pillows. In addition, there was a caged parrot and a xylophone that Aunt Cil was always proclaiming she would learn to play. Sitting regally beside her on the sofa was Sid, a huge scruffy tomcat she'd rescued from the streets, incongruously wearing a rhinestone collar.

"Champagne?" Seemingly out of nowhere, a maid appeared with a tray containing glasses, an ice-filled silver cooler and a bottle of imported champagne. She set everything on the table in front of Cil, then quickly disappeared. Without waiting for any response from her guests, Lucille reached for the bottle and filled Waterford flutes with the bubbling liquid. The ever present telephone, a Mickey Mouse model, was lying beside the cooler.

Brian remained standing. He shook his head when offered the drink, so Aunt Cil, undaunted, rose to place the glass on a corner of the marble mantel near his shoulder. He'd been casting questioning glances in her direction, but Zana was relieved that now he was giving his full attention to Cil.

"Where are they?" he said, his voice just this side of rude.

"Have some champagne, dear," Aunt Cil insisted. "Sit down and relax, then we'll talk about it." She gestured toward a chair. Aunt Cil's words were soothing, but Brian seemed poised to explode, so Zana was surprised to see him acquiesce to Cil's prodding by picking up the champagne glass and raising it to his lips. Still, he didn't sit.

"Where are they?" he asked again, his voice more modulated now.

"Honeymooners need a while to themselves. You know what they say—three's a crowd." Aunt Cil rubbed Sid's head, and the cat squeezed his eyes shut in contentment. "They'll be getting in touch with you in the next week or so, I'm sure."

Brian looked around in frustration, acting as if he could conjure them up from the woodwork. After long moments he spoke. "I can see you Zacharys all stick together." He set his glass back on the mantel. "You don't need to see me out, Mrs. Hebert. Thanks for the champagne." He walked to the front door and left. Zana was surprised he didn't slam the door behind him.

She got up from the love seat to look out the window. Brian was striding rapidly across the street, anger fairly emanating from him like heat rising from asphalt. She watched him stop and glance back at the house, then shake his head before climbing into a brown Jaguar and pulling away from the curb. Only then did she feel secure enough to turn around and confront her aunt. "Where are they?" she said, echoing Brian's query.

"Now, Zana . . ."

"Don't 'now, Zana' me, Aunt Cil. You know full well where they are. I can always tell when you're fibbing."

"I told no fibs," Lucille said coyly. "All I said was the honeymooners needed a little time to themselves."

"They're here, aren't they?" Zana headed for the staircase, just reaching the first step when her father appeared at the top of the landing.

"He's gone?" Russell asked.

"Yes."

"Good. Caroline isn't ready to face him yet. She didn't expect him to react like this." His relieved look told Zana that Caroline probably wasn't the one unwilling to face Brian.

"Tell her it's safe to come down," Aunt Cil called from the parlor. "We've got champagne to finish off, and Zana needs to get back to Natchez. It'll be dark before she's home as it is."

Well, that certainly puts me in my place, Zana thought. Allow me to have a drink with the happy couple, then cast me out. She returned to the parlor, uncertain how she felt about meeting her father's new wife, her stepmother. She took a large gulp of champagne to calm her nerves and almost choked on the fizzy liquid as her father entered the room, his arm around one of the loveliest women Zana had ever seen.

"Honey, I'd like you to meet Caroline." Russell seemed ready to burst with pride.

Caroline left the protection of his arm and walked across to Zana, giving her a soft kiss on the cheek. "Hello, dear. I've been looking forward to meeting you. I'm sorry you had to deal with Brian. I thought he was still in Europe and didn't expect him to get our message for a week or so. When I sent him a note suggesting he get in contact with you—to make sure you were doing okay with Russell gone—I had no idea he'd do it immediately." She took Zana's hands in hers. "I suppose I should have come down and talked to him." She looked at Russell.

"Now, honey, it wouldn't have done any good." He crossed the room and stood behind his wife, his hands resting on her shoulders.

Zana could almost understand how her father had fallen in love so quickly. There was something special about Caroline—her genteel loveliness, her calm Southern manner, her fragile appearance. She was tiny, barely five feet tall, with a smooth peaches-and-cream complexion and hair highlighted to a soft blond. She had the same green eyes as Brian, only hers were smiling, not glittering angrily, and there were tiny laugh lines around them.

But lovely stepmother or not, Zana couldn't erase her resentment at her father's hasty remarriage. Especially once she realized how much Caroline was like her mother—a blond version of the petite dark-haired Vivi. Zana knew her father was eagerly anticipating her blessing of their union, but Vivi had been gone such a short while, and it was too soon to expect her daughter to welcome a replacement.

"We'll simply have to give my son a little time," Caroline was telling Aunt Cil. "Russell's right. It's best not to confront him until he's had more opportunity to accept the idea. He'll come around eventually."

The look of concern on Caroline's face undermined her attempts to reassure the others. Zana, for one, wasn't buying any promises from a doting mother. From what she'd seen, Brian was an impulsive, ill-mannered boor. Probably always had been and always would be.

"Actually," Caroline went on, "Brian's been the one encouraging me to get married again, but I think he may have had his accountant in mind." She smiled lovingly at Russell, then turned back to the women. "That accountant of Brian's is a nice man, but I could never picture us together, especially after I met Russell." She giggled softly.

Russell reached out and took his wife's hand, looking totally smitten. Zana couldn't stifle the wave of sadness she felt as she watched the two of them. Caroline seemed to sense her mood. She reached out and patted Zana's arm. "I know this is difficult for you, dear. Forgive us for our impatience?" Her smile was an appeal.

"There's nothing to forgive, is there, Zana?" her father interrupted. "We must go on living. My daughter knows that."

Zana wanted to scream at him, to tell him she was in pain, but she didn't. It would only distress everyone, and there was no point in that. Experience had taught Zana life was too short for misgivings, that happiness was a fragile flower to be cherished during its existence. So she gave a weak smile which brought a big grin to her father's face.

He was obviously convinced he'd won her over, and for all practical purposes he had. She might be miserable, but she'd keep her feelings to herself and indulge her father—as always. Zana doubted, however, that Brian Westbrook would be so accommodating. Despite Caroline's prediction that he would get used to the idea of the marriage, Brian hadn't acted as though he would cool down quickly. Zana suspected he was going to do everything in his power to cause trouble for the newlyweds.

Zana left her half-full glass of champagne and bade the trio goodbye. Aunt Cil had been right. If she wanted to get home at a decent hour, she needed to be on her way.

"We'll stay here another day or so, then we're taking a Caribbean cruise," her father told her before kissing her cheek. "We'll call you from one of the islands in a few days, honey. Thanks for being so understanding."

After hugs and kisses with Caroline and Aunt Cil, Zana was finally on her way back home, depression setting in once she was alone. Where would Caroline and her father live? In the small house he and Zana had rented? And what would be Zana's place after the other woman moved in? The questions unnerved her. Zana wasn't sure she could face any more change.

CHAPTER TWO

AS SHE TURNED into her driveway, Zana saw the glare of headlights and Brian's brown Jag pulling in behind her. She got out of her car and watched as he climbed out of his and walked toward her.

"What do you think you're doing following me everywhere?" she demanded.

"Just making sure you got home okay. The way you drive, I wasn't sure you'd arrive back in one piece."

"Your concern is touching, but I'm quite capable of taking care of myself." What was Brian Westbrook up to now?

"You've probably had enough experience."

"What do you mean by that?"

"I'm talking about your thoughtless father. He'd better have more sensitivity for my mother than he's shown for his daughter."

"What gives you the right to speak ill of my father? I'm not listening to another word." She turned and began to move away.

"Your protective attitude toward that selfish gigolo amazes me."

Zana stopped dead in her tracks. She looked back at Brian and started laughing. She couldn't help it. *Gigolo? Her father?*

Brian studied her, apparently wondering whether she'd lost her mind. The expression on his face only made her laugh more.

A glimpse of Russell Zachary could have explained her laughter. He was a stubby five foot seven, with a bald pate surrounded by a fringe of gray hair. And a constantly expanding waistline. Hardly material for a ladies' man. Then there was his attitude. No, not Don Juan. More like Don Quixote, chasing windmills and dreams.

He loved books and music. His days in Natchez consisted of rising at dawn, listening to classical tapes, taking long walks, reading in the evening and retiring by ten. Zana had tried to get him to tutor a few students on the violin, but she'd had no success. Gigolo? The description was absurd. She wiped the tears of laughter from her eyes.

"I'm glad one of us finds the situation amusing," Brian grumbled. "Then again if a wealthy widow had just entered my family—" he flicked a disparaging glance at the modest house "—I might be a bit happier, too."

Zana gave him a look of disgust. "You're contemptible." She shook her head and started toward the house again.

Brian followed, calling from behind. "Maybe so. However, I suggest you don't start spending the bankroll just yet. My mother may be well off, but I control the purse strings."

So that was the problem. Brian Westbrook thought Papa married Caroline for her money. They were now on the front porch, and Zana was struggling with the key. Finally she managed to open the door and flip the switch to illuminate the darkened house. "Your assumptions about my father are ridiculous. Papa would never be so practical. It wouldn't even occur to him." She dropped her keys on the table and whirled to face Brian.

"Don't you think it's time you stopped defending him?" As the light cast a shadow on his rugged features, Brian's face showed a grimness that made him seem even harder than his words.

"With your tendency to prejudge, he'll need a lot of defending." Zana tossed her long hair away from her face. "Now, I'm quite tired. Why don't you just slink off and take that sorry attitude with you?"

He ignored her. "I suppose you saw them in New Orleans."

"And what if I did?" she asked defiantly. She might as well admit it. He'd probably find out eventually, anyway. And maybe if she answered his questions, he'd be satisfied and leave her alone. "They're planning to take a cruise," Zana continued, "and told me they'd phone from one of their ports of call."

Brian gave a quick snort. "I'm surprised he has enough money for a honeymoon—or is my mother picking up the tab?"

Actually she'd wondered about that, too. Russell had little cash, and Zana suspected the expenses would go on his credit card, with no thought as to how to pay them when the statement came. Cruises were costly—something else for her to worry about. Zana couldn't prevent tears from springing into her eyes. She turned her back on Brian and hurriedly brushed away the moisture.

His strong hands on her shoulders twisted her around. "Tears? Just the right touch. For a moment I felt a twinge of conscience for being too rough on you. But then I remembered you're a performer, able to flash a smile or switch on the waterworks at will. I won't forget that in the future."

Despite his words, his expression *did* indicate regret. And he was still touching her shoulders. Zana shrugged away from him. "If your memory's as bad as your people skills, I have nothing to worry about. Now, would you please go." She didn't want any sympathy from Brian Westbrook. He was an overwhelming man, too handsome for any woman's good, especially one as vulnerable as she was—especially in light of her father's elopement.

"As you wish. Where's the telephone directory? I need to find a place to stay."

"Here," she answered, moving into the kitchen. She lifted the directory from a shelf and handed it to him. Without a word, Brian accepted the directory and flipped it open.

Zana left him there and went to her room. She realized her behavior lacked any semblance of good manners, but doubted manners made an impression on him, anyway. Besides, she was under no obligation to that loathsome man in the entryway.

She removed her jewelry and wristwatch and kicked off her shoes, then stopped. There was no way she could change clothes while he was in the house. Zana gave a sigh of relief when she heard the car door slam. *Good. He's finally leaving and he didn't bother to seek me out to say goodbye.* She stripped off her skirt and blouse and put on a terry bathrobe.

When she headed for the kitchen a moment later to get a glass of water, Zana was shocked to see Brian coming through the front door with a brown leather briefcase and a garment bag.

"You're still here? I thought you'd left."

He silently took in her appearance, and she became aware of the fact that her robe was short, leaving a lot of leg exposed. "I changed my mind," he said. "I'm staying." He followed her into the kitchen, where he dropped into one of the cane-bottomed kitchen chairs and casually leaned back, hands clasped behind his head.

"You can't do that!" Zana was furious. "You *have* to leave. Tonight," she added for emphasis. Zana couldn't see anything good resulting from Brian Westbrook's being here.

"The Zacharys are a hospitable crew, aren't they?" he said sarcastically. "At least your aunt gave me champagne before showing me the door."

"She didn't. You stomped off."

"Well, maybe, but admit it—the two of you couldn't wait to see me go. Just like now. I'm surprised you didn't slam the door in my face." He leaned forward and placed an elbow on the table. "I think I'll just hang around until our parents arrive. Then I can talk to my mother and find a way to get her out of this mess."

"Mr. Westbrook, I give you my word they're not going to show up here. Not for a while at least. And I doubt that your mother feels a need to be rescued from any mess. So please make your call and go. I'm really not up to arguing anymore."

"I made my calls, a dozen of them. Every place for miles around is full. There's some kind of tour group in town and they won't be gone for days."

"You still can't stay here."

"Just try to get rid of me." His green eyes held a challenge. "I flew half the night to get home and then I traipsed around after you for most of the day. I'm beat and have no intention of driving to hell and back looking for some place to sleep. Anyway, my mother did say to check on you. What better way to do it? If you don't have a spare bedroom, I'll bunk on the couch."

Zana glared at him. "If you stay, then what?"

"Then wait for our parents. They may not show up tonight, but eventually they will, and I plan to be here. Russell Zachary is going to find out he's not just dealing with some lonely, impressionable woman."

"Are you telling me you intend to wait them out here?"

"Exactly." His voice was determined.

"But it'll be days, weeks maybe, before they return."

"So *you* say."

Zana sighed loudly, too exhausted to continue sparring with him. "Suit yourself, but you'll be whiling away the time alone. I'm certainly not going to keep you company. I'm going to Jackson in a couple of days."

Brian shrugged. "Perhaps I'll come with you."

"I don't think so." Zana glared at him. "The smart thing for you would be to return to wherever it is you came from until there's word."

"Memphis. But I'm not going back. Now that I've given it some thought, I realize I can't fulfill my obligations to you from there. No, for the time being, my home's right here.'' He walked over to the cabinets and began looking through them.

Zana put her hands on her hips. "But what about the neighbors? It isn't proper."

"It isn't proper for a big brother to look after his sister while their mom and dad are away on vacation? Surely the neighbors would approve." Brian's grin was close to a smirk.

"You're not my brother."

"It appears that I am. Stepbrother, anyway. Ah, here's the coffee." Brian pulled out a canister. "How about being a good girl and brewing a pot while I get the rest of my gear from the car?" He pushed the canister into her hand and headed back outside.

Just who did he think he was, treating her like a servant? Zana had half a mind to lock the door behind him, but he seemed obstinate enough to kick it in. She watched through the kitchen window while he set a suitcase on the porch and then returned to his car for another.

Apparently he hadn't gone home after his flight from Europe. Either that or he lived in his car. *He's moving in lock, stock and barrel,* Zana thought in disgust. How was she ever going to get rid of the man?

She walked to the door and flipped on the porch light, illuminating the small front yard. She couldn't have him tripping in the dark and hurting himself. If he twisted an ankle he might never leave.

He continued unloading the car. Zana wondered why he was bothering to bring in so much stuff. Surely after a day or so he would tire of this silly game. After all, Caroline had said he was a businessman with a company to run. He couldn't do it from her house.

That was only one of Zana's miscalculations.

"DO YOU ALWAYS SLEEP so late?" The draperies were flung open allowing a brilliant streak of sunshine to flood the room.

Zana slowly eased herself into a sitting position, the quilted bedspread dropping to her waist to reveal the top half of a sheer blue nightgown. She hastily pulled the comforter up to her shoulders. "What are you doing in here?"

"Keeping you from sleeping your life away." Brian set a cup of coffee on the bedside table.

Zana groggily rubbed her eyes. She'd lain awake half the night thinking about everything that had happened yesterday.

"I thought you had a job," he said.

"I do, but I don't need to leave until ten-thirty."

"Nice hours." He picked up the cup and handed it to her. "But I'm afraid it's still time to rise and shine, Sleeping Beauty. It's after ten now."

"Oh, my gosh!" Zana grabbed her clock radio, turning it toward her. Ten-fifteen! She started to jump out of bed, then remembered her uninvited houseguest. "Do you mind?" she grumbled.

"Since you asked so nicely." He gave her a tight-lipped smile, then turned and walked to the door, pausing to lean against the jamb. "Hope you won't expect breakfast too. I only do coffee."

"I don't eat breakfast."

"That figures," Brian said, glancing at her slim form beneath the covers.

Zana felt naked, as though she wasn't covered from neck to toe with a layer of bed clothes. Brian's gaze seemed to see right through them. "Please?" she asked, gesturing for him to go. This time he shrugged and left the room.

Despite a quick shower and a hurried attempt to find a clean outfit to wear, Zana couldn't help but notice how Brian had made himself at home. His shaving kit was on the vanity, his toothbrush in the holder and a hint of his woodsy after-shave lingered in the air. The small bathroom had already taken on a virile male feel.

After slipping into a pink jumpsuit, Zana hastily brushed her teeth and applied a bit of lipstick and blusher. Enough! she admonished herself, annoyed that she was so conscious of Brian's presence. As she crossed from bathroom to bedroom, she was stirred by the sight of him in slim-fitting jeans and polo shirt, at the kitchen sink rinsing out the coffee carafe. Why was he so at ease in her house, while she was turning into a wreck?

She decided to braid her hair at the studio. It seemed imperative that she put some distance between them immediately and get to a place where she could regain her equilibrium.

Zana wasn't used to men like Brian. Perhaps because she'd spent so much time with her father. Russell Zachary was quite a contrast to Brian—happy-go-lucky, pleasant, content to leave all practicalities to others. And her mother, immersed in her music, had had the same blasé approach to living. By necessity, Zana had been the pragmatic one.

From a very young age, she'd become accustomed to making most of the decisions. She'd been the one in control. Now, for the first time in her life, someone else was taking charge. That realization was not only unwelcome, but discomfiting.

She conducted her classes that day like an automaton. First there were a dozen four-year-old fledgling ballerinas, followed by a women's aerobics class, then a group of preteens. She finally finished at seven and took her usual route home, but because of weariness, gave scant attention to Zachary House.

Brian was at her home when she got there, more thoroughly ensconced than ever. The living room had become an office, containing a desk, a fax machine and a computer, complete with modem and printer.

"Where did these things come from?" He'd had a lot of luggage the night before, but his car couldn't possibly have held this much equipment.

"Hello to you, too," he replied. "I had it delivered from Memphis."

"But why? Surely all this stuff isn't necessary?"

"I wouldn't have bothered if it wasn't. Thanks to modern technology, I can keep in constant touch with my company and still be on hand when 'Dad' decides to return with my mother." He checked his watch. "You're late."

"Not really," she said, sinking onto the sofa. "This is my Tuesday schedule. Even though many of my students are on summer break, they still seem to prefer classes later in the day." She leaned her head back against the cushion.

"I'm about to fix myself a drink. Would you like one? A glass of wine perhaps?"

Part of her felt like barking at him for taking over her home and acting as if he owned the place. But another part conceded that it was rather nice to have someone wait on her—especially a man. As far back as she could remember, she'd always been the one fetching things for her father, never the other way around. And most of the men she'd encountered in the ballet world were pampered and expected star treatment.

"Maybe some iced tea?" she said. "There should be some already made in the refrigerator."

He headed toward the kitchen and returned a few moments later with a tumbler filled with ice and tea, which he handed to her.

Zana took a grateful sip. "Thanks, I needed this."

"I'm not much of a cook," he said, "but potatoes are baking and I picked up some salad stuff and a couple of steaks to throw on the grill. How do you like yours?"

"Medium rare," she answered, deciding that the man was full of surprises. He might be an uninvited guest, but he seemed to be trying to avoid putting demands on her. She cautioned herself not to become used to the special attention, however, since an unpleasant altercation between Brian and her father was probably going to occur, and whatever the outcome, Brian would leave.

Together they prepared the rest of the meal, and Zana began to relax a little. Perhaps she had misjudged him. Recalling her shock at the news of the marriage, she decided his earlier actions had most likely been the result of his own shock.

Now that he'd had a chance to calm down, he was behaving more rationally, just as she had. She dared not assume, though, that Brian was accepting the marriage; after all she really hadn't, either. But, at least, they had something in common.

They were seated at the wooden pedestal table in the kitchen, dawdling over coffee. He glanced at her as he added a splash of milk to his cup. "Do you miss the stage?"

"Sometimes," she said, surprised that he knew of her accident and retirement. It must have been in the American newspapers.

"Having your career taken away from you like that must be really tough."

Zana hesitated before responding. Since her mother's death, she'd become guarded about sharing her feelings. Her father had been dealing with his own loss and had been in no shape to take on her problems, too. Which meant she'd really had no one to comfort her. There'd been doctors who showed professional concern, but Zana's wounds had gone beyond dancing; it had been unbearable to think about her loss, much less discuss it with strangers. By the time she'd begun to realize her career was over, it had come with a sense of resignation.

Now she was feeling something else—hope. The possibility of having her career back. But she dared not mention that hope lest she tempt fate. "Leaving the stage was not an experience I'd want to repeat," she told Brian, using a flippant tone in order to put an end to his questions.

But apparently he was not easily deterred. "Did you always want to be a dancer?"

"Always. From my first lesson at age three I was hooked. I can't remember not loving ballet."

"And it seemed to love you back. You were becoming quite famous."

"I wouldn't go that far."

"I would, and that makes me wonder... What made you leave Paris? And before that, the Royal Danish Ballet?"

"It's not unusual for dancers to change companies," Zana said, offering an answer that really wasn't an answer. His probing made her uncomfortable. She wasn't willing to give Brian another reason to condemn her father. Because the truth was, the moves had been made for Russell's sake.

Her father had never stayed in one position long, which was probably just as well once his career began to wane. It meant he didn't end up being replaced by someone newer and better. Since it was important that her family stay together, whenever a move became imminent, Zana sought a new post— the dutiful daughter accommodating her father's wanderlust.

"But surely hopping from one company to another wasn't the best career strategy. Hadn't you just signed with Monte Carlo when the accident occurred?"

Zana studied him briefly. His information far exceeded that which would have appeared in any newspaper. "How do you know so much about me? I was never that well-known. Not in the United

States, anyway. It sounds as though you've had me investigated.''

"Not you. Your father. Naturally I learned a great deal about his daughter in the process." Brian got up to refill his coffee cup, then turned back to her. ''Let's get one thing straight. I'll not have my mother's heart broken by being dragged about from place to place. She's a nester. For years she's longed to have a home of her own. Now that I can afford it, nothing and no one will take it away from her. Certainly not some gypsy bridegroom. Russell Zachary's about to embark on a new style of living. Have I made myself clear?''

"Quite," Zana said stiffly. "What's clear is that without knowing my father—without even meeting him—you've assessed him—and not at all favorably.''

"I don't have to meet him to know plenty. His lifestyle has told me. Well, he can't have his cake and eat it, too.''

"What cake? What in heaven's name are you talking about?'' Zana rose and followed him across the kitchen.

"I'm talking about Zachary House. Obviously he thinks he can get it back simply by marrying my mother. But he's wrong. The price is higher than that. He's made his choice. Now he'd better be content to stay with her twelve months a year and pretend to be the happiest, most in-love man around. I'll not have her hurt."

"You . . . *you* own Zachary House?"

"Spare me the innocent act," he answered. "It won't work. You can protest all you want, but I know—and you know—Russell Zachary couldn't wait to marry my mother the minute he learned who'd bought the old mansion."

"What makes you think that? As I said before, you've never even met my father." Her protest now lacked some of its earlier conviction as she realized that anyone could have seen and misunderstood Russell's interest in the restoration of the estate. Her father hadn't attempted to conceal his curiosity, and while Zana had observed more discreetly, with Natchez being the size it was, any number of people might have spotted her, too. Including Brian. "It wouldn't be like Papa to take advantage of your mother."

"Oh, no? From what I've learned, it's exactly 'like Papa.' The man is an opportunist who thinks only of himself. And in this case, his actions definitely speak loudly. Zachary House was the reason for the elopement, my dear stepsister."

"You don't think it could have been love?"

"Especially not love." Brian laughed humorlessly. "Eventually you'll learn there's no such thing as love. Love is actually a social disease—a disease of illusion. Everyone has his or her own emotional agenda. It's just a lot easier to call it love." He set his coffee cup on the counter and left Zana alone in the kitchen.

She leaned against the cabinet, stunned by his comments. Could he possibly be right? Had her father married Caroline to regain his lost home? *No.* As she had told Brian, that wasn't like him at all. But in the back of her mind, there was a niggling doubt.

Russell had always been sentimental about the house, and for as long as Zana could remember, he'd filled her head with stories of his years there. Seeing the renovations had seemed to take him away from his present-day sorrows to the happiness of his childhood. No doubt Zachary House was where he'd first met Caroline, becoming enchanted with her in that special setting.

It was as though the old mansion had cast a spell over him. A spell that had proved to be contagious, with Zana getting caught up in its magic. Now she was getting caught up in something else, but it definitely wasn't magic. It was trouble.

THE NEXT DAY started off much as the previous one had. Brian awakened Zana with coffee, idling longer in her bedroom than necessary, leaning against the door frame, making her aware of him, then moving away and closing the door behind him.

It wasn't as if there'd never been a man in her life. Eligible males had always been around, but for the most part, she'd found being on stage with them more exciting. Dance had been the only romance of any consequence to her. There had been neither time nor opportunity for anything else. To stay on top in a world as competitive as ballet required absolute dedication.

Since coming to Natchez she'd dated a few times, but rarely more than once or twice with the same man. Recently she'd had several dates with Jeff Spencer, an orthodontist whose office was three doors down from the ballet studio. Jeff was young, available and nice. Unfortunately there was no chemistry, no tingly sense of anticipation like the one Brian Westbrook managed to create. The thought shocked her, and she couldn't erase the questions it aroused. What would it be like to kiss Brian? To feel his body against hers?

"Still in bed, little sister?" His voice was calling from the other room.

Sister. The word was a telling reminder of the way he saw her. A relative. A family member. And here she was having completely different ideas. Embarrassing ideas. The situation was getting out of hand, the close quarters causing flights of fancy. She had to force herself to return to reality. Work would probably be just the tonic.

Zana had just arrived at the studio office when the telephone rang. "I called your house to see if you'd heard from that heavenly man again." It was Aunt

Cil, her Southern drawl more pronounced than usual as she prattled on. "And guess who answered the phone? Himself," she said, responding to her own question. "This is perfect. Just perfect."

"Aunt Cil—"

"But we'd better not tell Russell and Caroline he's there. They left this morning—another reason I haven't called till now...first chance, you know. Now what do you think of Caroline? Isn't she perfect for Russell—sweet and delicate, just like your mother. But enough of them, tell me about Brian. Doesn't he just make you swoon?"

The conversation was typical of Aunt Cil. She always carried on a monologue, running her sentences together and hopping from one subject to another. And occasionally barking up the wrong tree, like now. Zana decided she'd better interrupt and set her aunt straight before she ordered wedding invitations. "If you have matchmaking in mind, I suggest you forget it," she admonished.

"But why? Money and looks are a rather nice combination, Zana."

"Brian isn't too fond of the Zacharys, or couldn't you tell?"

"Rhett wasn't always fond of Scarlett, either, but, oh, what sparks!"

"Quit trying to stir things up, Aunt Cil. If you were to mention potential romance to Brian, he'd probably echo Rhett Butler's 'I don't give a damn.'"

"Nonsense," her aunt replied. "He and I had a nice long talk about Russell and Caroline, and about you, too. He's a delightful boy—everything Caroline said he was."

Zana wanted to ask more about the "nice long talk," especially the part about her, but decided it was best she didn't know. Aunt Cil had probably tried everything short of bribery to fob her niece off on Brian.

"Caroline says he's rather jaded about *amour*. Seems that when he was in college he fell in love with a girl and asked her to marry him. She said yes, then dumped him for a wealthy fraternity boy. Broke his heart. Of course, now women trip all over themselves wanting to be his wife, but he's become cynical. Probably just needs the right woman to change his attitude."

"Aunt Cil, please don't."

"Please don't what, dear?"

"Don't try to start something between the two of us. The last thing I need is Brian deciding I'm after him. He's already convinced Papa is a fortune hunter. He'll think it's a family trait."

"Why, Zana, I wouldn't dream of such a thing." She sighed loudly. "Now, if all you're going to do is complain, I'll ring off. Tell Russell and Caroline hello for me if you hear from them."

That night Zana stayed at the studio late, attempting to postpone the confrontation she was sure she'd have with Brian regarding her aunt's call to the house. First she worked out—the self-imposed routine designed to hasten the return of her leg to its former strength. After the exercise, Zana rested, then deliberately dallied—going over her books and tidying up. On the way home she stopped at a fried-chicken place and purchased a meal for two. It was almost nine when she arrived at the house.

Brian was hunched over the computer when she opened the door. He turned around, rubbing the back of his neck. At first he didn't speak, but his wary look said a lot. Aunt Cil's interference had carried exactly the message Zana had feared it would.

He eyed the take-out sacks. "Dinner? Or should I call it a bedtime snack?"

"Look, Mr. Westbrook, you're the uninvited guest, so consider yourself lucky to get food in any form and at any time."

"I'll try to remember that." He switched off the computer and rose to take the bags from her. "Hmm, fried cholesterol."

"Are you always this sarcastic? Or do you have a good side?"

He rubbed his neck again and gave her a sly smile. "Actually, this *is* my good side." He sniffed the contents of dinner. "Doesn't smell half-bad. We might as well eat since you've brought it."

"I'm not hungry anymore," she said, irritated by his continued sniping. "You go ahead."

"But eating alone's no fun."

"You should have thought of that before you decided to be so unpleasant."

"Didn't mean to growl. The damn computer just ate two pages of figures." He sounded almost conciliatory.

But if that was Brian's idea of an apology, it didn't mollify Zana. Frustrated or not, he ought to have been appreciative of her gesture rather than making snide comments. "I've got to get packed," she said, in an effort to put him off. "I plan to leave tomorrow right after my morning classes."

"Oh, yes. Jackson, wasn't it?"

"That's right. It's the last weekend of the International Ballet Competitions."

"Hmm," he said. "Is that the real reason, or could that be where the lovebirds really are?"

"I'm beginning to wonder if you're completely insane," she snapped, the outburst surprising even herself. "How many times do I have to tell you our parents won't be back for at least another week? They're not in Jackson, and I'm not meeting them there, or anywhere. Why would I want to? Why would they want me to?"

Brian continued to look disbelieving.

"Okay! Waste your time skulking around here like a stubborn hound, but I've got better things to do."

She flung her purse over her shoulder and headed for the bedroom, grateful for the chance to get away from him. The man was intolerable. And to think her father had married his mother. She could only pray there wouldn't be many family reunions in her future; she didn't want to be thrown together with Brian Westbrook any more than she already had.

THE LOBBY of the recently renovated hotel, a landmark on Capitol Street, was buzzing with people when Zana checked in. The hotel stood only a few blocks from the Jackson Municipal Auditorium where the Ballet Competitions were being held, and most of the other guests were dancers, teachers, choreographers, directors or critics.

The ballet world had moved to Mississippi during these past two weeks of June. It was here young dancers, who were destined to be the future stars of ballet, would be discovered. Even in the hotel lobby there was an undercurrent of tension and guarded optimism.

Zana had a couple of brief but enthusiastic reunions with old friends, then, with a bellhop following, made her way up to her room. The bellhop unlocked the door and stepped back to allow her entry. Zana stopped short. Instead of the simple room she'd had the week before, she was staring into a lavish suite.

"I'm sorry," she told him. "There must be some mistake."

He looked at the key. "No, this is correct."

"But..." She was about to continue the argument when a connecting door opened and Brian appeared from the next room.

"Well, isn't this a coincidence? We seem to have adjoining rooms." He handed the bellhop a couple of dollars and ushered him out the door.

"Coincidence, my big toe," Zana said as the door closed. "You set this up. Don't bother trying to deny it."

Brian looked at her, one eyebrow arched. "I've decided to take care of you, remember? So here I am. Now, wouldn't it be a wonderful surprise if Mommy and Daddy joined us?"

Zana exhaled loudly. "It's a good thing you're not a professional sleuth. You wouldn't have enough money to restore *my* house, much less Zachary House if you had to depend on your deductive reasoning for an income. Our parents are in the middle of the Caribbean, not here. Trust me."

He leaned back against the closed door and shook his head. "I don't think so."

Zana wanted to scream. Was she never going to get rid of this man and his suspicions? She walked over and took hold of his arm. "If you've had enough accusing for today, then it's time to go back into your room and play with your computer. I don't have the patience for this now."

"I didn't bring my computer along."

"Pity. Then you'll just have to find something else to occupy your time. I have plans for this weekend." She nudged him toward his door.

Brian smiled down at her. "Sounds fine to me. I'll just tag along."

"No way. There are people here who know my father, and I don't particularly care to continue this warfare with you in front of them."

"But you won't have to. We'll sign a nonaggression pact and the marriage will be our little secret." Brian made a cross-my-heart gesture.

"How will I explain you, then?" Zana's frustration was increasing. "And don't tell me to say you're my big brother. All my friends know I don't have a brother."

"Then we'll just have to tell them I'm your lover."

"What if my *lover* is the one I'm concerned about explaining your presence to?"

Brian wrinkled his brow. "That *would* make it rather sticky. But I don't think there is a lover. You were never really serious about that English dancer, or you wouldn't have left him. And since no one else has come along to take his place, I'll be the man in your life for the moment."

Brian knows about Kurt. She felt her face redden. "You certainly left no stone unturned in your investigation."

"I believe in being thorough. But all I had to do was read the gossip columns. According to them, the two of you carried on a sizzling affair." Brian took her by the arms and pulled her close. "Were they right, Zana? Did he make you sizzle?"

"That's none of your business!" She wrestled free. "Why don't you just go back to Memphis?"

"You're no more hospitable here than you were in Natchez. But you might as well relax, because I'm not about to leave." He placed his hands on her shoulders and turned her toward her bedroom. "Now I suggest you change. We'll go to dinner in an hour or so."

Zana went to her bedroom and closed the door behind her. She wished it had a dead bolt to offer a real barrier to him. She didn't doubt that Brian would be charging in within the hour if she didn't reappear.

Actually she *had* planned on calling Kurt and spending an evening reminiscing. Because the Englishman had been her most frequent dancing partner, the ballet world had assumed they were a couple and then gossiped about every detail of what they considered a tempestuous romance. But the wagging tongues had been wrong. What had been tempestuous was not the romance, but Kurt himself.

As a ballet star, he wasn't accustomed to women spurning his advances. To Zana's knowledge, she was the only one who had, and therefore she became maddeningly desirable to him. He continued to pursue her with a vengeance, throwing frequent tantrums to try to bully her into submission. Zana suspected that if she'd ever given in, Kurt would have lost interest.

Still, she liked him. When he wasn't petulant, he was charming and entertaining. But she wasn't in love with him. She never had been. And for Zana, love was a prerequisite for sex. Kurt had never understood "her archaic Victorian attitude," as he called it, and the two had endless discussions about the subject. During the past weekend in Jackson, he'd been attentive and unusually patient—biding his time no doubt. Zana guessed that this weekend he'd be expecting more. Perhaps it would be better if she dined with Brian. Both choices were depressing.

CHAPTER THREE

BRIAN EFFORTLESSLY maneuvered his sleek car through the early-evening traffic until pulling into the parking lot of an Italian restaurant near the Ross Barnett Reservoir. "They've got great fettuccine. The pasta's homemade."

As usual, Brian had taken charge. Zana didn't argue. Mainly because she was starving, and the wonderfully pungent smell of garlic and olive oil that assailed her nostrils as they entered the restaurant squelched any objection she might have had.

Brian ordered antipasto and a bottle of Chianti, and then they sat rather self-consciously while waiting for their food.

"You're staring, Mr. Westbrook," Zana said finally.

"Is that a crime? As I'm sure you know you're a very beautiful woman."

"Oh? Actually your scrutiny makes me feel as though I have something caught in my front teeth. I'd pull out my compact to check, except we haven't eaten yet."

"I would think you'd be used to being watched, being a performer and all."

"It's a bit different when the audience is in a darkened auditorium below you, not two feet away."

The arrival of the antipasto ended that conversation, which was a blessing as far as Zana was concerned. Brian's unexpected compliment had made her uncomfortable. She found him easier to deal with as an adversary.

They discussed the food and chatted about the restaurant's decor. Then with the main course—sautéed veal scallops with lemon, accompanied by fettuccine with Parmesan cheese—the talk moved on to the weather.

Brian ate heartily, prodding Zana to have another bite every time she put down her fork. "You're too thin."

"A job qualification for my line of work."

She thought he was going to argue, but instead, he went back to his own meal and stopped pressuring her to eat. All of a sudden his mouth curved in amusement.

It was the first time Zana had seen a genuine smile from him. "What's so amusing?" she asked.

"I still have that image of our parents peeking through the French doors on your aunt's balcony," he said. "Like two mischievous children hiding from the grown-ups."

"You knew they were there? Why didn't you come back in and confront them?"

He sobered. "To tell the truth, I was beginning to feel like a first-class heel. There was my own mother unwilling to face me. I really regretted losing my temper." He shook his head.

"They do so want our approval. My father was practically begging me to tell him it was okay."

Brian's eyes hardened. "I didn't mean to imply it was okay. It's not." He leaned toward her. "All I said was I regretted losing control. I haven't changed my mind about anything. And I repeat, I will not see my mother hurt."

For an instant Zana had almost begun to like Brian. Now she wondered why. He was completely pigheaded. She couldn't tolerate his uncompromising attitude.

"Don't look so worried." He patted her hand. "I'm not happy about this marriage, but I won't behave like a raving lunatic again. Promise." He actually smiled again. Zana's body responded with an unexpected rush of tingles as her resolve to remain indifferent left her. She reached for her wineglass, hoping her hand wouldn't shake.

"Did you manage to get any work done this week?" she asked, attempting to change the subject.

"Surprisingly, yes. But, thanks to my trip, there's still some things to catch up on."

Zana watched the waiter refill their wineglasses. "Just what is it you do?"

"I'm a consultant."

"And what do you consult about?"

"Computer viruses," he said. "I've got a small company in Memphis, but I plan to relocate everything to Natchez once Zachary House is finished. I travel a lot because I've got contracts with businesses all over the world, so it doesn't really matter where headquarters is—as long as it's near an airport."

"Computer viruses. From what I read that's a lucrative field right now."

"It pays the bills," he said almost indifferently. "And I fell into it quite by accident. I majored in computer science in college, then went to work for a large firm. But I didn't like someone else telling me what to do, so I took a chance and started my own business. Luckily it worked out."

"Any other family? Brothers and sisters?"

"None. My father's dead and you're my sole sibling."

"Cute." She lifted her glass and drank more wine.

"Is there anything else you'd like to know? Ask away."

Zana decided she might as well make the most of the opportunity. She knew so little about the Westbrooks, even though her life was now bound to theirs. "You must have been pretty successful—from college to your own company in what? Ten years?"

"Thereabouts. I'm thirty-two, if that's what you're asking. My life has really changed since I was a teenager from the wrong side of the tracks. Back then, when friends and I passed Graceland, I'd brag that someday I'd buy my mother a big house like that. It was tremendously important. Probably more to me than her—maybe because she didn't think it would ever happen."

His words brought all sorts of questions to mind. Questions Zana knew she dared not voice. Brian hadn't been well off in his youth. Was that why he was suspicious of her father's reasons for marrying Caroline? "Still, you did it. But why Zachary House?"

"One of the companies I was working for had picked up the estate from a defaulted loan. The company president mentioned that it was a lovely old place but sadly deteriorated. That piqued my interest, and I decided to come down and have a look. I liked what I saw and bought it."

Zana didn't know what else to say. If she asked too many questions about the house, Brian would be even more convinced that she and her father had conspired to get it. She was rescued when the waiter arrived with their desserts and coffee.

"Would you like to visit the old homestead?"

"What?"

"Zachary House. Would you like to see it?"

How could she resist? Despite everything, she wanted to wander through the rooms where her father and grandfather had grown up. "I'd love to." Zana smiled warmly.

"Then it's settled. We'll go as soon as we get back to Natchez."

BRIAN TOOK ZANA'S ELBOW as they moved down the aisle toward their seats for the awards gala. She was dressed in an orange chiffon evening gown, and he was wearing a tux—Zana had no idea where he'd found it on such short notice, but she was glad he had, and that he was at her side. Much as she hated to admit such a thing, even the presence of an irritating new companion was preferable to sitting through the performances alone. She'd welcomed this challenge, but at the same time feared it, worried that she might not be able to handle it.

"I had no idea the Competitions were such a big deal," Brian whispered in her ear.

"They aren't particularly well-known except to those devoted to ballet. Yet stars like Baryshnikov and Marakova have competed and won medals at these events."

"And Zana Zachary," he added. "In Moscow, wasn't it?"

She smiled. "Maybe you're not such an inept sleuth, after all."

The lights dimmed, and Zana was soon lost in the spectacle that followed, dancing in her mind every bourrée and pirouette with those on the stage. The music wrapped itself around her and she was transformed from the damaged and scarred Zana into the Zana who had brought even demanding European audiences to their feet.

By the first intermission she was emotionally drained, choosing to remain in her seat while the rest of the audience went to the lobby. Brian took her hand as the curtain went up the second time, and she found his action surprisingly consoling. But that only lasted a short while, and when Kurt danced the final pas de deux with his new partner, Alexa Bereskova, a sharp pain pierced Zana's heart.

Brian continued holding her hand, giving her the strength to sit through the ovations. When the house lights came on, he leaned toward her as she blotted her damp eyes with a handkerchief. "You okay?" he whispered.

She nodded.

"Do you want to leave?"

"There's a party... I've agreed to attend."

"You don't have to."

"I think I do," she said.

"What the hell was your father thinking when he let you come to this alone? He should have been here."

Zana stiffened, wishing that Brian hadn't witnessed her vulnerability. It gave him another excuse to attack Russell.

The hotel ballroom reverberated with chatter as Zana and Brian made their way into the middle of the dense crowd. They had returned to the suite first to allow Zana to repair her makeup and regain her composure before facing more reunions and memories.

A local bank honoring the participants in the competition had provided a lavish buffet for the guests. From a passing tray, Brian lifted two champagne-filled glasses and handed one to Zana. He appeared totally relaxed, in contrast to Zana, who still felt decidedly unnerved.

Some of the performers were beginning to drift in; the arrival of each star caused a murmur to rise from the crowd. Many of the dancers sought Zana out, and as she and Brian went through repeated introductions, she experienced a jumble of feelings: happiness at seeing old friends and acquaintances, envy of those still dancing and desire to win back the position she'd had to abandon. Added to that was the stress of coping with Brian's presence.

It had been comforting having someone at her side; explaining him was another matter altogether. For convenience, she'd begun to introduce him as her cousin from Memphis. But each time she did, Brian, to her consternation, would say, "Kissing cousin." Fortunately he'd offered no demonstration.

When the room suddenly burst into exuberant applause, Zana knew that Kurt had arrived. He stood framed by the doorway, waving and nodding to acknowledge the crowd's reaction, and Zana could tell he was enjoying all the adulation. He looked wonderful in a dark jacket, pink silk shirt and paisley cravat. He was the only man she'd ever met who could wear a cravat without looking pretentious.

One of his dramatically arched eyebrows rose when he saw her. Then he strode in her direction, effortlessly kissing a hand or cheek along the way, and within a matter of minutes, he stood before her and Brian.

"Zana, my darling," he said, pulling her into a fierce hug and kissing each cheek. "Why didn't you call me? I was afraid you'd changed your mind about coming this weekend."

Embarrassed by the attention they were attracting, Zana freed herself from his grasp and turned to introduce Brian. She didn't know what to expect from Brian, but the look on his face told her not to use the cousin comment.

"Kurt Rutherford, Brian Westbrook."

"How do you do," Kurt said to Brian, extending his hand for a limp handshake. He lowered his voice. "And who *is* Brian Westbrook?"

"Zana's escort," Brian answered, placing an arm around her waist.

Zana couldn't believe what was happening. She could understand Kurt's challenging glare. He wasn't used to competing with other men. But what was behind Brian's behavior? Was he baiting Kurt? Probably just being obnoxious, she decided. After all, that was Brian's forte.

"Actually a newly acquired relative," Zana interjected. "My father's remarried, and— But I'm sure you don't want to hear the details now. You'd miss greeting the rest of your adoring public."

"Rubbish," Kurt retorted. "You know my eyes are only for you." He took Zana's hand, pulling her toward him again. "Russell married—that's wonderful. That means it's easier for me to make you an offer—something I've been thinking about all week. Can we meet later?"

Zana felt uneasy. It was a familiar sensation, one she always had when Kurt wanted to be alone with her. "The hotel coffee shop?" she suggested.

The dancer laughed. "Will you never change? Always playing mouse to my cat. No, for our discussion, I prefer the privacy of your room. So quit teasing and tell me where to find you."

Zana scribbled the room number on a piece of paper torn from her program, then cast a quick glance at Brian as Kurt slipped the paper into his pocket. She was tempted to smile, knowing Kurt's goal of getting her alone would be thwarted by Brian's presence. There was amusement in Brian's eyes, yet Zana noticed that his jaw seemed clenched. Kurt's, too.

"Until later, darling." Kurt kissed her hand, before moving off to greet someone else.

"I can just imagine his 'offer,'" Brian scoffed. "Fortunately I'll be around to act as chaperon."

"I don't need a chaperon," Zana protested, feeling exasperated by both men. "Just get me out of here."

She was glad that when they reached the suite Brian went immediately to his own bedroom. At least he'd provided her with some time alone before she had to see Kurt again. She had to wonder if her former partner really thought he'd get further tonight than he had in the past.

He hadn't suggested as much a week ago, yet she couldn't help but be suspicious when Kurt was overdoing the charm. She smiled to herself as she looked into the mirror. If Kurt was expecting romance, then he was in for a disappointment. Her feelings for him hadn't changed, and she was certain they never would.

Whatever Kurt's intentions, she knew he wouldn't stay once he discovered Brian was in the next room. And that was fine with her, because she wasn't sure Brian would be polite enough to leave them alone.

She really had no desire to mediate a confrontation between the two.

She learned quickly that her concerns were totally unfounded. Kurt's proposal turned out to be more professional than personal. He'd accepted a position as artistic director of a new company in London and was simply inviting her to be on his staff as a teacher.

"I wanted to ask you last weekend, but figured there was little chance of talking you into leaving Russell. Now there's no reason for you to refuse." He put his hands on her shoulders. "It could be a wonderful new life, Zana—not the spotlight, but still the world you know. And it could develop into something more—if you wanted it to."

She eased out of his embrace and crossed to the window. Kurt's image was reflected in the pane, and she studied it for a few moments. He was leaning casually against the bar and seemed assured that she'd agree.

Zana wondered how he could be so confident when she didn't know the answer herself. Most women would have jumped at his offer, so why hadn't she? It would solve a lot of problems and give her part of her old life back. Yet as much as she wanted to say yes, a part of her told her to refuse. She turned to him. "I didn't expect this. I'm honored, flattered . . . I just . . ."

"You're not going to say no to me, are you, Zana? You seem to make a habit of that, my darling."

She shook her head. "I don't know. Everything's changed so quickly, Kurt. My father. My life." She didn't tell him she was thinking about trying to return to the stage. As long as performing was an option, it was her priority. "Could I have a little time to think it over?"

Kurt walked over to her and caressed her cheek. "Of course." He smiled. "As long as you eventually agree, I'll give you all the time in the world. Call me when you reach a decision. I promise not to pressure you."

She gave him a look of disbelief.

"Not much, anyway." He smiled again, then turned and left.

Zana was on the couch, her arms around her knees, her soft chiffon gown flowing around her when Brian came in.

"Your visitor left early."

"Did you have your ear glued to the door?"

"No, I tried the old glass-to-the-wall trick, but it didn't work. I couldn't hear a thing."

She looked up at him. "Kurt offered me a job. In London."

"Are you taking it?"

"I don't know. I can't decide."

"Then I'll help you out—tell him no. The man's in love with you. Since you don't love him back, neither of you would be happy working together."

Zana suspected Brian had overheard more than he'd admitted. "I remember your saying there's no such thing as love."

"True, but some misguided individuals insist on believing in it, anyway. Rutherford *thinks* he's in love, so, for all practical purposes, he is."

"Interesting analysis. But hardly reliable coming from a cynic like yourself."

"I'm a realist, not a cynic."

"Whatever." She shrugged. "Your attitude's still negative and callous. And now, before you think of a snide retort, I'll say good-night." She got up and started toward her bedroom.

"Sure you don't want company in there?"

Zana didn't even turn around. "If I did, I'd have invited Kurt to stay." She slammed the door behind her to punctuate her response.

While she prepared for bed, Zana pondered Brian's last comment. Obviously he was joking, but it wasn't the first time he'd almost...almost what? She wasn't sure she was ready to know the answer.

THE PHONE WAS RINGING when Zana arrived home in Natchez, with Brian right on her heels. She rushed from the hall into the kitchen to answer and heard

Brian pick up the extension he'd had installed in the living room.

"Baby!" her father's voice greeted her. "How are you?"

"We're fine," Brian answered, before she could respond. "Are you and my mother enjoying the cruise?"

Zana's father cleared his throat. "Yes…of course. Here, I'll let you talk to her."

"Hold on a minute, Mr. Zachary." But Brian was too late; Russell had already passed the phone to his new wife.

"Brian, honey, what are you doing in Natchez?"

"Overseeing the work at the house. I looked in on Zana as you suggested, and she was kind enough to invite me to stay here." Zana pulled the cord to its full length, so she could give Brian an indignant stare. But he was in no way intimidated, and meeting her gaze, openly dared her to contradict him.

"Brian, I'm sorry I didn't discuss this with you beforehand," Caroline said. "I would have told you earlier, but it was a rather spur-of-the-moment thing. I'll have to admit Russell and I got a bit carried away. But we couldn't help ourselves. We love—"

"Mother, don't apologize to me," he interrupted. "I only want you to be happy. You are happy, aren't you?"

"Very. Oh, you're such an understanding son."

Zana rolled her eyes. If his mother only knew the depths of Brian's understanding.

"Now we'd better let Zana and Russell talk a moment," Caroline said. "'Bye, dear."

"'Bye, Mother."

"Zana?" Her father's voice was wary, as though he expected to hear Brian's voice, instead of hers. But Brian was no longer on the line. She could hear the rustle of papers and then the soft clicking of computer keys from the other room.

"Yes, Papa," Zana answered. "When do you plan to be home?"

"We're to arrive back in Miami on Friday. We'll stay over for a few days, then catch a flight to New Orleans. Maybe spend the night at Cil's before returning to Natchez. I'll call and let you know for sure. Is everything okay?"

"Everything's fine," Zana fibbed. There was no use telling him that Brian had taken over her home and her life. If she did, her father might never come back. Besides, complaining would only make her father and Caroline miserable, not get rid of her intrusive guest. "Don't give me another thought," she added. "Just enjoy the rest of your honeymoon. See you soon. 'Bye now."

"'Bye, honey."

Zana was replacing the receiver when she looked up to see Brian only a few feet away. Apparently he'd been listening, after all. *We might as well have it out right now,* she thought, bracing herself against the cabinet, ready for battle. But the anticipated barbs never came. Instead Brian silently went to the refrigerator, grabbed a can of fruit juice, then went back to his computer.

Zana stood at the living room door and watched him for a few seconds before deciding to turn on the television set. She was tired but too restless to sleep. A half hour in front of the TV would help her unwind.

Brian had other ideas. He turned away from the computer and stared at her. "Do you mind? I'm trying to get some work done here."

"As a matter of fact, I *do* mind. This is *my* house, *my* living room, and *my* television set. You wouldn't have to be catching up on work if you hadn't followed me to Jackson."

Zana realized she was being difficult, that in fact the weekend would have been horrible without Brian's support, but she preferred to return to their adversarial relationship. All the way back from Jackson he'd been in her thoughts.

She'd continued to wonder about the flirtatious remark he'd made after Kurt had left, even going so far as to imagine what would have happened if she'd told him she *did* want his company in her bedroom.

Beneath his quarrelsome demeanor was a mystifying man who'd managed to both unsettle and intrigue her. He was frequently rude to Zana, yet he treated his mother with concern and sensitivity. He seemed anxious to conceal his caring behind a wall of hostility.

Unless she was careful, Zana knew she could easily get carried away by her feelings for Brian. It was obvious she was still emotionally bruised and in need of self-protection. "If the TV bothers you, please feel free to leave," she said, adding for good measure, "surely there are some rooms available in town by now."

Brian studied her briefly. "Oh, no. You're not running me off with a little noise. I like sharing your home and hospitality. So just go ahead and watch your precious television show, and I'll work, anyway." He returned his attention to the computer.

A little noise, huh? Zana flipped through the channels in search of something truly annoying. A situation comedy—not bad, an incessant laugh track—but maybe there was something louder. Cable news, uh-uh. Public broadcasting, definitely not. Too quiet and dignified. Ah, what was this? A war movie. Perfect. Plenty of gunfire and mortar blasts. Zana nudged up the volume with her remote control as the U.S. Navy began blasting a beach with artillery.

Brian looked over a couple of times, and Zana smiled to herself, hoping she was distracting him. Then he stood up and moved closer to the television, staring at the screen for a few moments, frowning. Suddenly he snapped his fingers and smiled. "Now I've got it—*Sands of Iwo Jima.* John Wayne." He joined her on the couch. "This is a classic. One of his best."

Zana eyed him warily. "You've seen the movie?"

"About two or three times. But I can never get too much of the Duke. One of my favorite actors of all time. They don't make them like that anymore." Brian leaned back and propped his feet on the coffee table. "This is too good to miss."

"But your work..."

"It'll keep." He tucked a sofa cushion behind his head.

Damnation, she thought. *What have I done to myself?* She didn't really like old movies, especially old war movies. Now she was stuck. It was either sit here and suffer through the film, or leave and as much as admit to Brian that she'd been acting childishly. Never. She'd stay. It was two hours later when the final credits rolled and Zana reached for another tissue to dab at her eyes. The movie *would* have to be a sad one.

"Glad you didn't get too caught up in the film," Brian said smugly.

"I don't know what's wrong with me. I haven't cried this much since... since my mother died."

Brian gently patted her shoulder. "It takes a long time to work all the tears out. I cried buckets the year my father passed away."

"When was that?" Zana turned her head to face Brian.

"I was just a kid, about eight. Dad had been sick for a long time. But it didn't make losing him any easier. After he died, my mother had to go to work to pay the medical expenses and everything. She was totally unprepared and had no job skills. She started as a maid, then became a waitress, but there were always too many bills and not enough money. We eventually lost our house and had to move to a garage apartment in Memphis. But somehow we managed to survive, and with luck and scholarships, I got through college."

"I thought you said your mother was an heiress."

He frowned. "I don't believe I used those words. She's wealthy *now,* because of some solid investing. This may sound immodest, but I seem to have a talent for the stock market. Early on I acquired a lot of holdings in her behalf. Do you want to know what stock and how much, or has your father already shared all the details?"

Zana felt her face redden in anger. She looked away, trying to control her temper. Everything had been pleasant for a few minutes. Why did Brian always have to spoil the moment? "I doubt you'll believe it," she said, "but I'd never heard your name or your mother's until she'd already married my father. And I know next to nothing about either of you. Perhaps I should have engaged an investigator, too. Then questions wouldn't be necessary."

A slight smile played around his lips. "Good point."

But Zana was not easily mollified, and a sense of irritation lingered. "Well, good night," she said. "It's been a long day." With that she left the room, taking the box of tissues with her.

In bed, she reflected on their evening together, not knowing what to make of him. Until he'd become suspicious again, he'd been quite companionable. Another side to his personality. How many had she seen so far? There was the combative Brian, the domineering Brian, the seductive Brian, the thoroughly objectionable Brian. And each of those facets was completely unpredictable. With Brian, she often felt as jittery as she did on opening night. But she also felt more alive than ever before.

WHEN SHE AWOKE the next morning, Brian had gone, a note on the cabinet explaining he'd left for a few days of business meetings in Memphis. Apparently, the phone call from his mother had assured him he could safely make the trip before her return to Natchez. Zana read the message, sad that he'd forgotten his promise to show her Zachary House. Then she saw the postscript at the bottom of the page: "We'll take that tour as soon as I get back." He hadn't forgotten after all.

During the next few days the house seemed empty. Zana felt lonely, an emotion previously unknown to her. She'd learned to be her own companion at an early age. Even though she had often accompanied her parents on tours, there were times when she couldn't go along and had remained behind at school.

She'd become adept at finding things to do— reading books, playing solitaire, doing crossword puzzles or needlework. Even after the accident, when she'd no longer filled her hours with practice, she'd kept busy.

But now nothing held her attention for long. During the day she ran errands, taught her classes and continued to strengthen her knee. And, as always, she took the long way home so she could monitor the progress on Zachary House. But she continued to feel at loose ends. There was no one to visit, no girlfriends to meet for lunch. Her nomadic childhood had prevented her from forming lasting friendships.

She wished Brian would call. Even a curt conversation with him would be welcome. But she didn't hear from him, nor from many others. The phone rang only three times: first Lucille, then Jeff inviting her to a movie and finally a wrong number. Zana talked to Aunt Cil for more than an hour, attempting to change the subject every time Cil mentioned Brian, which was often. When they finally said goodbye, Zana felt drained, as though she'd been through a ten-hour dance rehearsal.

Which might have been why Zana agreed to see a movie with Jeff. She knew it was a mistake, even as she hung up the phone. But she couldn't back out now. What excuse could she give? She couldn't tell him the truth—that she was falling in love with someone else.

Now where did that ridiculous notion come from? Zana shook her head fiercely, the unwelcome thought making her glad that she'd agreed to go out with Jeff.

Zana was feeling disgruntled when Brian returned late Saturday night. She was in bed trying to force herself to concentrate on a book when she heard his car pulling into the driveway. The key she'd given him clicked in the lock, and she listened while he made a trip back to the car to retrieve his belongings.

There was a tap on her door, then Brian opened it. Zana's bad mood vanished as soon as she saw him. She thought he looked wonderful. Wonderful, but tired. Stubble shadowed his face. He wore no tie, and the sleeves of his rumpled white shirt were rolled to his elbows.

He smiled at her. "So, did you miss me?"

"You've been gone?"

Brian laughed and crossed the room to sit on the side of her bed. Through the cotton sheet, Zana could feel the warmth of his body next to hers. Neither spoke, and for endless seconds, green eyes stared into blue.

Suddenly Brian straightened. "I'm dead on my feet—better hit the sack. See you in the morning." He stood and headed toward the door. "We *are* still going to see the house?"

Zana nodded, grateful for the distance he'd put between them. For one crazy moment she'd considered inviting him to stay with her. It was a relief when the door closed behind him.

CHAPTER FOUR

ZANA WAS TOO EXCITED to dawdle over coffee; instead, she quickly downed a cup so that they could be on their way. After years of listening to her father's reminiscences about the Zachary estate, she was finally going to see it. Not just a surreptitious glimpse from the window of her car, but a personal guided tour.

Even though Russell had willingly given up his birthright when he'd chosen to pursue a career in music, his heart had never really relinquished ownership. The mansion was an important part of his history, having been in the Zachary family for more than 150 years, passed down from father to eldest son, ever since Matthew Zachary had commissioned its construction in the nineteenth century.

First to inherit was Matthew's son, Randolph, then Randolph's son, Clyde, the chain of father to oldest son broken only when Russell went against his father's plans for the trailer company.

Russell had always insisted he'd made the right decision, and had her mother still been alive, he probably wouldn't have returned to Mississippi. But Vivi had died and with her had gone Russell's intense devotion to music. So he came home—although home as he'd known it was no longer there.

Brian unlocked the gate and drove the car up the weed-choked brick drive. Since it was Sunday, the construction crew wasn't present, leaving Zana and Brian alone. She looked around the grounds expectantly as they climbed the steps to the front door. The house bore a similarity to another Southern mansion, the famous Stanton Hall. Both had large white columns, dark shutters and two-tiered porches.

"I plan to call the landscapers in immediately after the exterior is finished," he said. "The bricks in the drive should be relaid, and those weeds and scraggly bushes have to go. A few of the trees are dying, but I think the magnolias and live oaks can be saved. I want to put in lots of azalea bushes to add some color, too."

"The place is going to be beautiful. Your mother will really enjoy it here."

"She already does. She's an avid gardener. There was once a big rose garden around back. Mother intends to restore that herself."

What a labor of love, Zana thought. During her convalescence, she had discovered an affinity for growing roses. There had been a couple of neglected peace rosebushes in the backyard when they'd come to Natchez. She'd nursed them back to health and added a tropicana and a Mister Lincoln. She envied Caroline's huge garden.

Brian unlocked the door and gestured for Zana to precede him. She hesitated, then crossed over the threshold and stood transfixed, staring at the entry hall. "It's lovely. Everything I imagined."

"The painters are nearly finished in here," Brian said. "They put on the second coat this week. All that remains is staining and varnishing the floors."

"What will you do about furniture?" The entry was bare, except for an exquisite crystal chandelier hanging directly over them.

"A few things left over from the sale are being refinished. I've found a couple of earlier pieces, and I'm trying to find more. I want to decorate with authentic nineteenth-century furniture."

"Wonderful." Zana fingered the molding around the frame of the front door, then pointed to the right. "And what's in there?"

"Ah, the music solarium. Come with me." The hardwood floor caused their footsteps to echo around them. "A grand piano for my mother is going to be my next purchase. She started taking lessons a few years ago, but only has an old battered upright. I can't wait to surprise her with a new one." Brian took Zana through each room, explaining both its earlier function and what the Westbrook family would use it for.

She was familiar with much of what Brian was telling her and impressed with the depth of his knowledge. Obviously he'd done extensive research on this house and its former residents. He knew almost as much from public records and books as she did from Russell and Cil's stories.

Some rooms were more complete than others, but basically Zachary House looked only a few weeks away from occupancy. Zana felt a stab of jealousy at the thought of Brian's moving into this fine old home. And what about her father? Since he and Caroline were married, it appeared the two of them would be living here, too.

Brian had stopped making snide comments about Russell, but seeing the house rekindled her own doubts. *Did* her father have ulterior motives in marrying Caroline? Zana wanted to deny it, but wandering through the house, she couldn't dismiss the notion from her mind. In his youth, her father had walked away from his family, from his heritage. Zana knew he had regrets—he'd voiced them frequently since their return to Natchez. Had he seen Caroline as a way to regain what had once been his? Zana hoped not, prayed not.

Again it occurred to her that decisions about her own future would have to be made soon. Russell didn't need her as caretaker or companion any longer, so she was free to do as she wished. The thought was sobering, yet invigorating. For most of her life, she had served two masters: ballet and family.

Now she had only to take care of herself. She could stay in Natchez and continue to teach. She could accept Kurt's offer and go to work in England. She could even attempt to dance professionally again. The options seemed limitless to Zana, a woman who'd never really had choices.

"I'm going to leave you alone for a few minutes," Brian said, interrupting her musings. "There are some things in the attic I want to check on."

"Fine with me."

"By the way, if you go upstairs, you'd better stay in the west wing. The carpet layers haven't finished in the east side—Mother's side—so it's like a mine field what with all the tacks and tape and carpet remnants."

Brian's absence gave her some time to drink in the grandeur of the empty rooms. She made another tour of the ground floor, then headed upstairs, going from room to room, avoiding the unfinished areas and finally stopping to stare wistfully through the window of the master bedroom, at the deep green leaves of a huge magnolia. She opened the window and inhaled the fragrance of the tree's enormous ivory-colored blossoms.

The setting brought back her father's stories about Matthew Zachary. Of his arrival in Louisiana from Rhode Island only a few years after the Battle of

New Orleans. How he fell in love with Lisette, the daughter of an aristocratic French Creole family, and brought her to Natchez, to the new house they'd built together. Lisette had probably walked through the house just as Zana had today, contemplating the placement of each piece of furniture, each fixture, then dreaming about the children they'd have.

Zana strolled through a couple of the bedrooms again, then started for the hall wondering what had become of Brian. It had been more than twenty minutes since he'd left her. What could be so interesting about the attic? She stopped in midstride as she spotted him at the top of the landing, examining a portrait that had been propped up on a sawhorse next to a wall.

He turned around as she approached. "Do you know who she is?"

Zana froze once she got a better view of the picture. Except for the hairstyle and clothes, it could have been a painting of her. Russell and Aunt Cil had always said she favored her grandmother. Having seen family photographs, Zana had agreed, but now she realized how strong the resemblance actually was. It was almost as though she had dressed for a masquerade and was looking into a mirror.

"That's my grandmother—the one I was named after."

Zana briefly looked at Brian then returned her gaze to the painting. The figure in the portrait had black hair like Zana's, but rather than the casual braid her namesake wore, her hair was pulled to the side of her neck, spilling over the front of her blue satin dress. Her eyes, the same shade of blue-violet as granddaughter, stared back at Zana.

Zana gently touched the edge of the ornate frame. There was a deep crack in one corner and the surface was scratched and dented. "Wherever did you find it?"

"I didn't. It was among the odds and ends the contractor discovered in the attic during the planning phase. There are other family portraits and photographs up there, too. You're welcome to have a look. This one caught my eye, though, and I thought you'd like to see it." He moved away from her and started down the stairs, pausing midway to comment, "The resemblance is startling, isn't it?"

An understatement. Zana reached out to touch the frame again, feeling as though her life had somehow been altered by this unexpected connection to the past. Her mother, born in Belgium, had lost all of her family during World War II. And except for occasional visits from Aunt Cil and her cards and letters, Zana had no ties to anyone but her parents. Seeing herself reflected in her grandmother's image, suddenly gave her a greater sense of belonging.

She turned to find Brian standing at the bottom of the stairs looking at her strangely. Descending the steps, she stopped before him, and he reached out to stroke her cheek, then, almost in slow motion, he pulled her into his arms, his lips meeting hers, coaxing her to return his kiss.

Zana's hand curled around the newel post. She'd never experienced anything like this before.

Slowly Brian slackened his grip and lifted his lips from hers. His eyes held hers. "You kissed me, too, you know," he said, after a long pause.

Zana stared at him in utter surprise and confusion. She didn't speak. She *couldn't* speak.

"Well, you did."

She continued to gaze at him, feeling completely muddled.

"Don't waste your time waiting for an apology," he said, his tone defensive. "I'm not the least bit sorry. It would have taken a saint to resist you." Then he took her into his arms and kissed her again, but released her almost immediately. "And as you can plainly see, I'm no saint."

With that, he strode away and disappeared out the front door, leaving Zana gaping after him. Who was the crazy one here? she wondered. Him? Her? Both of them? The man was a walking paradox, and every minute she spent with him confirmed just how complex and complicated he was.

He was leaning against one of the massive white columns, as Zana came out the door a few moments later. She wasn't certain how to act after their kiss. Should she say something to him? Or simply go to

the car? She opted for the latter, but Brian grabbed
her elbow as she passed. His eyes were solemn, almost hard. "I don't suggest you read anything into
that," he told her gruffly.

Zana raised an eyebrow. "I'll try to keep myself
under control," she shot back, hoping that flip-
pancy would mask her confusion.

"Well," he said, "I can assure you it won't happen again." He turned his back to her, pulling the
front door closed, then checking the lock.

Zana walked to the car. Once inside, she snapped
on her seat belt and faced straight ahead. The
friendship that had begun between them had vanished with that unexpected kiss. How was she going
to endure Brian's presence now?

Zana was angry—mostly with herself. She
shouldn't have allowed him to kiss her, and she
should never have kissed him back. What was it
about Brian Westbrook that put her in emotional
quicksand, her ability to escape impossible?

Instead of driving her home, Brian announced that
he'd made brunch reservations. Zana really didn't
want to be in his company, but he hadn't bothered to
ask for her opinion. Going along with his plans
seemed easier than protesting and possibly revealing
how much his kiss had unsettled her. Besides, being
at a restaurant with him was preferable to being alone
with him at home.

"I'll be leaving this afternoon," he announced after they were seated at a window table. The restaurant was a converted mansion and their table offered a view of the formal gardens. "I have a business appointment in Gulfport first thing in the morning, then I'm heading back to Memphis."

She looked at him, unsure of how she felt about this news. "For how long?"

"Indefinitely."

Zana fell silent.

"Do you have a problem with that?" Brian asked. "I thought you wanted to be rid of me."

She set the menu down. "I don't understand, that's all. What about our parents? They're due back before long. I thought you didn't want to be away when they returned."

"I can wait."

"This is unbelievable!" Zana threw her hands in the air. "You come to my studio searching for them, follow me to New Orleans, then to Jackson..." Noticing she was beginning to draw an audience, Zana lowered her voice. "You move into my home, and now you're moving out. Just like that!"

"Surely you'll agree it's for the best, especially after what happened back at Zachary House." A fleeting smile crossed his face. "Or is that why you're making such a fuss about my leaving? Were you envisioning a second Zachary at Zachary House? If so, I suggest you make other plans. There'll be no more

Zachary-Westbrook weddings. I'm not nearly as gullible as my mother."

"Why you...you egotistical jerk! I'd rather sleep with a pig than marry you."

Brian smiled again. "Charming comparison. Sounds like your Aunt Cil talking." He paused. "But then, she seems to consider me *very* marriageable."

"Leave my aunt out of this. If she's dropped hints about your being groom material, it's the result of her mistaking you for a nice person—the kind she'd like to see married to her niece. I'll be sure and clear up any delusions she has the next time I speak with her."

"Hostile today, aren't we?" he chided. "Miffed that I'm not going along with the program?"

"I don't know why you're so obsessed with that idea. Don't forget, Mr. Westbrook, *you* kissed me."

"And you didn't exactly struggle to get away. In fact, I got the distinct impression you were hoping for more."

Zana pushed her chair back and threw her napkin onto the table. "I'm not hungry. Let's leave."

"Well, I *am* hungry, so you might as well relax. I have no intention of missing lunch just because you're pouting over your plans going awry."

"The only plans I have as far as you're concerned involve getting my privacy restored," she hissed. "I find your outrageous arrogance harder and harder to take."

"Funny, you didn't seem repulsed when you were nibbling at my lips so provocatively."

"Brian Westbrook, you are undoubtedly the most objectionable man I've ever met."

She was surprised when he started to laugh. "Thank you," he said. Then he signaled for the waiter and ordered omelets for both of them.

Zana sat mutely through the rest of the meal, occasionally taking a bite of her omelet, mostly gazing out the window. She felt ready to explode with frustration. Their conversation had made no sense whatsoever.

"I don't know what you're so upset about," Brian said after the waiter brought the bill.

"I'm not upset, I'm—"

"You've been complaining that you want me out of your hair," he interrupted. "You're finally getting your wish, although I'm tempted to argue that the lady doth protest too much. Now if you're finished, shall we go?" He scribbled his name on the credit-card slip, then rose and helped her from her chair.

Neither of them spoke on the short trip to Zana's house until Brian steered the car into the drive and switched off the ignition. "Don't get too used to my being gone," he said. "I'll be back after our parents return."

Zana started to make a caustic reply, then thought better of it, realizing she was glad he was leaving.

Lunch had provided no respite from her jumbled emotions. Being apart from him would give her a chance to try to deal with everything that had happened.

Brian went through the house, stuffing a briefcase with folders and packing his shaving gear and a laundered white shirt into a small overnight case. He took the luggage to his car, then returned for a suit in a garment bag. "I'll send someone down in a few days to move all my office gear to Zachary House. You have my card, so if you need me, my staff in Memphis can find me."

"I tore the card up. Besides, what could I possibly need you for?"

With a grimace of exasperation, Brian took out another business card and attached it to the refrigerator with a magnet, then walked out the door.

Zana had trouble sleeping that night. The wind was moaning through the trees as if despairing that there was no man in the house. Unsuccessfully trying to erase Brian from her mind, Zana finally fell into slumber near dawn, not awakening until after eleven.

Since she had classes to teach that afternoon, she hurriedly made her bed and dressed. It had become her habit to practice before the students arrived, and she wanted to make sure she had enough time for the workout. Today, however, the effort seemed wasted.

Instead of concentrating totally on the exercises, her thoughts kept straying to Brian.

She started over, attempting to focus on the effect each stretch had on her body. Her goal was to improve her strength and flexibility with every workout. But even analyzing her movements didn't help.

Zana couldn't understand it. Never before had any man taken her attention away from ballet—it had always been the other way around. She shook her head, hoping to regain her perspective. Relaxing her grip on the bar, she repeated a series of arduous dance movements.

The physical activity gave her few problems. Even her knee was ceasing its rebellion. At first, whenever she'd exerted any extra pressure on her injured leg, a sharp pain would remind her of its limitations. But the healing had progressed to a point where she could execute an occasional *grand jeté* or *tour en l'air* with little physical penalty.

There'd been definite improvement over the past few months. She wasn't imagining it. And the improvement encompassed more than just a lessening of pain. She was also regaining the strength and finesse necessary to be a soloist.

After the accident, Zana had accepted her doctors' opinions that she'd never dance professionally again. Now her recovery was allowing her to believe that the medical experts had been wrong. And that meant it was time to see a specialist in New Orleans to get another assessment. She'd put it off, fearing that the Louisiana doctors would only confirm what she'd already been told. But the weeks of avoidance had to come to an end. If the prognosis was the same, she was merely back where she started. Except that now she had other options.

ZANA WALKED OUT of the orthopedist's office into a New Orleans shower. But she didn't cover her head, didn't rush to her car. What difference did a few raindrops make when she'd been given her leg back? After innumerable X rays and considerable poking and probing, Dr. Neiman had confirmed her own suspicion. Yes, she could dance again. How well? He couldn't say. Only time could provide the answer. But the opportunity to be a ballerina was hers once more.

Surprisingly Zana felt more satisfied than elated. A few weeks ago, this news would have sent her in search of a celebration. Now, too many other things had happened, and this just added to the confusion.

She needed to talk to someone. Since Lucille was expecting her after the appointment, she drove her car over to the familiar town house.

"Come in, hon," Cil said. "I've got some iced coffee waiting." Today her aunt was wearing a bold fuchsia caftan, large dangling fruit-shaped earrings and gold wedgies on her feet. She motioned her niece into the living room. Sid was lying on one of the love seats watching Zana as if daring her to move him. Zana wasn't about to mess with the big tomcat, so she took a chair instead.

"Okay, tell me everything," Aunt Cil commanded as she filled tumblers with cold black coffee followed by sugar and rich cream.

As Zana recounted the doctor's words as they drank, Cil smiled happily at the news. "That's wonderful." She patted Zana's hand enthusiastically. "How come you're not jumping for joy or something? I thought this was what you wanted."

"So did I." Zana plucked at the hem of her skirt. "Maybe it hasn't sunk in yet. Or maybe because there's so much going on now, I'm just confused."

Aunt Cil studied her intently. "What do you mean, going on?"

"Oh, you know. Father's marriage. Caroline and Brian."

"Ah, yes, Brian. This sounds interesting. The two of you were alone in Natchez... Tell me what happened."

"Nothing happened," Zana insisted. "If you recall, I said *Caroline* and Brian." She met Cil's scrutinizing gaze defiantly. Give her aunt an inch, and she'd have you in church, wearing a white dress.

"I don't think Caroline's the problem," Cil said. "Looks to me like my niece may have finally found herself a man. Didn't I tell you he was something special? I'll bet it was love at first sight."

Zana stood up. "Oh, Aunt Cil, don't be ridiculous," she protested, even though her aunt wasn't completely wrong. Zana had never believed in love at first sight, but if she was honest, she'd have to admit her heart had skipped a beat or two that first rainy day at the studio and every time she'd thought about him since.

And she couldn't deny that for a moment during their kiss at Zachary House she'd imagined the two of them together for a lifetime. Had more than her body been injured in the accident? Maybe there was some sort of delayed reaction affecting her thought processes or attacking her common sense. Because one thing was certain—Brian did not have the same feelings about her. He'd made that painfully clear.

Had he realized what she was thinking? Did it show on her face during that lunch? Obviously he'd noticed something. Why else would he have wasted no time telling her that there wasn't going to be *another* Zachary-Westbrook marriage?

The tinkle of ice cubes which her aunt was busy adding to her glass, brought her back to reality. She accepted the offer of more coffee and changed the subject to Russell and Caroline. Fortunately Cil was willing to let the topic of Brian drop, and there were no more discussions about him for the rest of the afternoon and evening.

Zana left for Natchez early the next day and headed straight for the studio. When she eventually arrived home, the telephone was ringing. She'd missed her father and Caroline by a few hours; they were calling from New Orleans and planned to be in Natchez by six o'clock.

Zana rushed around straightening the house, then went about preparing dinner. She welcomed the labor as a way of keeping her thoughts off Brian. Fortunately she'd shopped the previous week and had plenty of food on hand, including the ingredients for her specialty—bourbon chicken. The festive dish would make a perfect welcome-home meal.

The house was neat and the chicken simmering on the stove when the slam of a car door announced the arrival of Russell and Caroline. Zana hurried to greet them.

A few moments later, as she watched her father across the dinner table, Zana thought he looked great. He was tanned and rested, and the pain she'd grown accustomed to seeing in his eyes was no longer there. He even laughed out loud a couple of times. Caroline was obviously good for him.

"You should have seen your father in the conga line," Caroline giggled softly, winking at Zana. "Of course, I had to practically browbeat him to get him to dance."

"Browbeating must run in the family," Zana muttered to herself.

"What, dear?"

"Oh, nothing. Tell me more about the cruise."

"We had a lovely time. Danced every night. Once I finally got Russell out on the floor, he was magnificent, a wonderful dancer. When we waltzed, it was heaven." Caroline placed her hand on his and squeezed it. "Now tell us what's been going on here? What do you think of Brian? And where is he? I expected him to be around, but when I called his office, they told me he was on a business trip to Nashville."

"I'm sure he'll be back soon," Zana said, then she tried to change the subject. "How long have you two known each other? Tell me about your courtship, Papa."

Zana watched her father run a finger around the edge of his collar and wondered what was wrong. Russell had always been one to avoid problems. Was he worried that this time he'd blundered into a problem—Brian Westbrook, to be exact—that couldn't be avoided?

Finally Russell spoke. "I suppose one could say I was trespassing at Zachary House." He glanced up at Caroline and seemed to receive a sudden infusion of confidence, because his head rose and his voice grew strong. "As you know, I hadn't been inside in almost forty years. I saw the workmen and hoped to have a peek without the owners knowing. But Caroline happened to be there, too. She was such a vision. I thought I was dreaming."

"Fortunately for me, you were wide awake." Caroline commented. "And your timing was perfect. You popped in on the same day I had driven down to check on the carpenters for Brian." She smiled and turned to Zana. "Anyway, Russell came in, we introduced ourselves, and he asked me to lunch."

"I think we knew right then that we'd end up married," Russell said, taking Caroline's hand in his.

"But when did you manage to be together? I mean, without my knowing?" Zana asked.

"That wasn't hard," Russell admitted. "You always rushed off to the studio in the morning, Zana. You were never around to notice I was seeing anyone. While you were at work, Caroline and I were having late lunches and taking walks around town every day. Nothing fancy. She may have had me out on the dance floor every night during the cruise, but for the most part I prefer the quiet life. I had enough excitement all those years I was performing."

"Anyway," Caroline continued, "after a week I had to return to Memphis, but then Brian left for Europe and I was lonely, so I came back to visit Russell. We just picked up where we left off—with our lunches and sight-seeing. Like your father, I'm not a night owl. In fact—" she glanced at her watch "—it's getting late already." Caroline got up from the table and started clearing away the dishes.

"I'll take care of these," Zana said.

"Oh, no," Caroline said. "I'll help you."

"Not tonight." Zana made an effort to sound firm. "You both must be tired from the trip."

"Well, if you don't mind, Zana," her father said. "Caroline did say on the way home that she was weary. We'll be getting to bed."

Nevertheless, Caroline made three more trips to the sink with dishes before Russell could pull her away. The woman was definitely not the meek little female Zana had originally thought her to be. But then, all she'd had to go on was Caroline's appearance and Brian's protective—apparently overprotective—attitude. Pleasant as she was, Caroline seemed to be a take-charge sort of person, a trait she'd obviously passed on to her son.

"Good night," they said together.

A half hour later Zana was washing the last of the pots and pans, still musing on the evening. Russell certainly seemed happy. But there was something else about him, something indefinable. It wasn't merely the renewed vigor. There was an added spark, a glow in him she'd never seen before. She placed the drying cloth on the drain tray and caught her frown reflected in the kitchen window. At the moment, Zana wasn't sure how she felt about her new stepmother. Or her changed father.

CHAPTER FIVE

ZANA FELT AS USELESS as a third mitten now that her father had married. Caroline had happily taken over the job of caring for Russell which required some getting used to. Caroline was always busy cooking, cleaning, running errands, checking on the work at Zachary House.

Russell seemed to feed on her energy. He tagged along to look at the renovations, assisted in the kitchen and even started playing his violin again, often accompanied by Caroline on the old upright piano that had arrived on the truck sent to retrieve Brian's computer.

After a few days, Zana decided Caroline was truly a steel magnolia. Beneath her delicate facade was a tungsten core. Zana had always admired women with grit—women like Aunt Cil. But with Caroline, the admiration was colored by unsettling feelings of resentment.

Although her stepmother did as much as possible to include Zana, her efforts didn't work. Zana liked Caroline, but she missed her mother and wasn't ready to accept someone else in that role. Especially someone who was so different from Vivi. Her mother had been quiet, almost introverted, and frequently ill with headaches or bouts of the flu. Caroline had an apparent zest for life and a hardy constitution.

So in self-defense, Zana stayed away from home as much as possible, going to the studio earlier and remaining later. There was no real reason for her to still be upset by the marriage, yet irrationally she was. It didn't help that she often had to witness the couple billing and cooing like a pair of lovebirds.

Her escapes served another purpose, too. With most of her students on vacation, the studio was usually empty. Each hour of extra practice reinforced what her doctor had told her. The corrective surgery after the accident had been more successful than anyone could have foreseen. Now that she knew she could perform again, the only question was whether she wanted to badly enough.

Zana had been convinced that, given another chance, she'd choose to go back to the stage. But for the first time, she wasn't so sure. Had the forced retirement lessened her desire to perform? Or had the desire truly been there? Maybe her ambition hadn't been her own, but rather her parents. Dancing continued to bring her joy—unbelievable joy, but did loving dance mean she had to perform for others?

Did she really want to be a soloist? A prima ballerina? Despite the doctor's assessment, Zana didn't really know how much her knee had healed. She was able to do some difficult movements, but occasionally her knee would stiffen or threaten to buckle. And she was reaching for the aspirin bottle a little too often. But physical problems aside, Zana had to wonder, too, if she still had the drive, the edge needed to achieve success. If it had been lost, and she resumed performing, then Zana risked being relegated to the corps.

A glance at the wall clock warned her that it was after six. Russell would soon call to check on her. Zana smiled at the thought. Her father's solicitousness was something new, attributable, no doubt, to Caroline. With Caroline being such a natural caretaker, Zana was amazed that she could have raised a son as . . . difficult as Brian.

Surprisingly, Brian hadn't reappeared in Natchez. Their respective parents had been back almost a week, and it annoyed Zana that Brian—who'd been so hell-bent on confrontation—had remained out of sight. Some pressing business matter must have kept him away. Caroline obviously knew, but she volunteered no information, and Zana didn't want to ask. In fact, she was relieved that she didn't have to deal with his prickly presence, along with everything else.

Apparently Caroline had talked to him, though, because her conversation was sprinkled with ''Brian said this'' and ''Brian said that.'' Sometimes Russell joined in the discussion, miraculously able to mention Brian's name now without blanching. It seemed that Caroline had even been able to give her husband a strong dose of resolve as far as his new stepson was concerned.

As Friday approached, Zana decided to call Aunt Cil and invite herself to New Orleans for the weekend. From a couple of remarks Russell had made, she'd guessed that Brian would show up in Natchez Friday or Saturday, and she preferred to be gone when he did.

Russell might feel up to facing Brian, but Zana wanted to be miles away when he returned, not at all anxious to witness some kind of showdown between the two. She also hoped to avoid the confusing emotions that surfaced every time she thought about their kiss at Zachary House.

A weekend in New Orleans would be a perfect time to sort out her feelings about Brian and her father's marriage. However, when she called the town house, Zana discovered her plans had been thwarted. Cil wouldn't be home; instead, her aunt was coming to Natchez.

"I CAN'T WAIT to see the old place," Cil said breathlessly as she embraced Zana. The two had pulled into Zana's driveway one right after the other late Friday afternoon and were making their way to the front door. In Cil's hand was a carrier containing Sid. "Caroline's told me about the changes. I wonder if it's the same as I remember. I understand Brian has shown you through Zachary House already. What did you think? Is it what you imagined? Did you like our old home?''

"Zachary House is lovely," Zana said, finally able to get in a word. "And the renovations are exciting. It's almost like history reborn," she continued, hiding her surprise that Brian had told his mother he'd taken her to see the house. Considering their embrace at the bottom of the stairs and their subsequent discussion, Zana felt certain he hadn't provided *all* the details of their visit.

They entered the house, and Cil hugged both Russell and Caroline before making herself comfortable on the couch. She pulled a hat pin from the back of an outlandish flower-bedecked straw hat, which she removed and laid on the coffee table. Sid, finally released from his confinement, glanced around haughtily, then jumped up beside her.

"When can we go over?" Cil directed her question to Caroline.

"Anytime you want," Caroline said. "Brian's moved in and he's there now—Russell and I took him some lunch about eleven. He's been overseeing deliveries all day. We can tour the house, then the darling should be free to join us for dinner.''

Darling, my foot! Zana was ridiculously hurt that he was in Natchez and hadn't tried to contact her. She was also annoyed that no one else had told her he'd arrived. Apparently the meeting between her father and Brian had already taken place, and she hadn't even been aware. Zana had no time to ask any questions or examine her feelings further because Cil was taking Caroline at her word.

"How about going now?" Her aunt, even more excited than before, hurriedly replaced her hat on her head and stood up.

"Fine," Caroline agreed.

Russell, who'd started reading while the women talked, immediately put down his book and straightened his tie. Zana continued to be surprised by her father. She could have sworn he'd been concentrating on what he was reading. Yet the moment Caroline indicated she wanted to leave, he'd responded like a dozing pup springing into action at the sound of the word "walk."

The man who for the past year had been unhappy and preoccupied was definitely gone. Perhaps Caroline was exactly what he needed. But even as Zana thought that, she felt as if she was betraying her mother's memory.

The four of them got into Aunt Cil's new Cadillac Eldorado and made the short trip to the old Zachary estate. Zana sat in the back, thinking about Brian and trying to ignore the chatter between Cil and Caroline. She was still upset that he hadn't called or made a point of seeing her, but she knew that was foolish. Brian's stay in Natchez after the wedding hadn't been for the purpose of being with her, but merely a way to ensure that his mother was safe and happy, and not in the clutches of some parasitic fortune hunter. He'd said nothing that would give her reason to think otherwise.

They pulled up to the gate at Zachary House and turned in. After her tour with Brian, Zana had purposely avoided traveling by the mansion. Now she was surprised at how much had been accomplished since that visit. There was a new brick drive, and workmen were installing a sprinkler system for the lawn.

Brian came out the front door as they stopped the car. Zana had wondered how appealing he would seem after their time apart. Would he really be as handsome as he was in her imagination? The answer was yes.

If anything he looked better. He wore chinos and a teal pullover that complemented his eyes. She was pleased she'd taken the trouble to change from her shorts and T-shirt into a white linen skirt and a black-and-white patterned blouse. *Not that it makes any difference,* she told herself. *He'll either fail to notice, or decide I'm dressing to entice him.*

Not only had she not forgotten Brian's good looks, but she'd started to soften toward him. However, it wasn't long before he angered her once more. It began with his giving her a perfunctory peck on the cheek—one of those insipid social kisses she'd grown to abhor during her performing days. Then with false politeness, he ensured she was included in the conversation and took her elbow as he guided the little group from room to room. The whole act was enough to make her want to grind her heel into his toes and tell him what she thought of his hypocritical perfect-host routine.

Perhaps the worst part was the way he watched her. Like a suspicious store detective, she decided. Was he worried she was going to steal the silver?

"Oh, how wonderful," Aunt Cil enthused, clearly oblivious to the tension between Brian and Zana. "You've put the petticoat table exactly where it used to be."

Zana recognized the table. It had been in the upstairs hallway at Cil's town house. One of the few family heirlooms she'd managed to hang on to after the bankruptcy, she'd apparently made a gift of it to Brian.

"It's just like I remember. My grandmother and great-grandmother used it to check their hemlines." She did a little twirl, clicking the heels of her sandals together as she inspected them in the full-length antique mirror.

"When are you going to have a housewarming, Brian? You must have one, you know." As usual Cil was dominating the conversation, and Zana was surprised that Caroline didn't try to compete.

"I hadn't really thought about having a party," Brian answered, gesturing to the others to proceed him up the stairs.

"Oh, but you *must*. It would be so—" Cil stopped in midsentence. "No, no, no. This isn't the place for Mama!"

Zana saw that her grandmother's portrait hung on the wall beside the landing. The frame had been repaired and the canvas had undergone some restoration.

"It was always in the master bedroom, Brian. You have to put it in there."

"Yes, dear," Caroline said. "Cil's right. If we're trying to achieve historical accuracy, we should hang the portraits in their original places."

"Don't you remember this one being in the master bedroom, Russell?" Cil asked.

He nodded. "Hanging opposite the bed."

"Then that's where it must go now, in your bedroom. Don't you agree, Brian?" Caroline prompted, her eyes twinkling. It was clear she recognized the resemblance to Zana, but she didn't comment on it.

For the first time since she'd met him, Zana actually felt sorry for Brian. She could just imagine how he relished the notion of that portrait facing his bed. But unless he wanted to make a scene, he was trapped. As if to confirm her suspicions, he silently grasped the frame in his hands and lifted it from the wall.

Followed by the others, he obediently entered the bedroom and leaned the painting against the wall Cil had indicated. "Excuse me while I hunt up a hammer and hangers."

As Brian left the room, Caroline turned to Cil. "Come see what we've done to your old bedroom." She, Cil and Russell headed out the door, leaving Zana to herself.

When she'd been in the room before, it had simply been the master suite. Now it was *Brian's bedroom* and her imagination was threatening to go wild. The focal point was a big feather bed covered with a satin burgundy spread. A marble fireplace, over which her grandmother's portrait would soon hang, graced one wall and a large wardrobe the other. Suddenly, despite the fact that she knew it was absurd, she had the strongest compulsion to get as far away from this room as possible.

The fates weren't kind enough to allow her escape, though. When she casually tried to wander out, she collided with Brian. He grasped her arm to steady her, and Zana felt as if she'd been burned. He must have shared the sensation, because he let go of her immediately.

Since she was blocking his way, she stepped aside to let him enter the bedroom. Leaving was no longer an option—the others were returning. But at least she and Brian wouldn't be alone. She couldn't possibly go too soft in the head with all these people as witnesses.

As she watched Brian, his work coached by the other three, Zana's thoughts went back to their physical encounter of only moments ago. She had to admit, if only to herself, that she hungered for his touch. It made no sense, and she wasn't happy to acknowledge it, but she longed for him to kiss her again.

Once the portrait was hung to everyone's satisfaction, Caroline suggested they have dinner. Zana could think of nothing more unappetizing than a cozy family meal, and from the look on Brian's face, the idea appealed to him even less. But he had as few alternatives now as he'd had with the business of the picture, so with an obvious air of resignation, he courteously escorted them down the stairs and out of the house, on the way suggesting a new restaurant.

All through dinner—a Southern meal of grilled catfish, turnip greens, fried green tomatoes, black-eyed peas and corn bread—Brian seemed distracted. Yet he made every effort to be gracious and charming as Caroline and Cil asked him question after question about the house. When they'd finished quizzing Brian, both women began talking nonstop, the other three giving up any pretense of joining the conversation.

Zana tried to envision the choreography for *Four Seasons* while silently humming Vivaldi's score. The ploy had gotten her through many a tedious fund-raising dinner. Tonight, though, it wasn't working. She was finding it impossible to ignore Brian.

Zana listened and spoke only when addressed directly. She was amused when Caroline began talking about Brian as if he wasn't there. "When he gets an idea in his head, it's almost impossible to change it. He becomes so stubborn. I've learned it's best not to argue. Of course, he's usually right. Zachary House, for instance. I didn't think he should buy it." She smiled at Russell and took his hand. "But I'm so glad he did."

Zana watched Brian. How did he feel about Zachary House now? Did he still see it as Caroline's dream home, or as the reason his mother had become involved with a gold digger like Russell? If ideas stayed fixed in his mind, as Caroline said, would he ever accept his father-in-law? Or Zana herself?

She remembered how he'd looked when they coerced him into hanging the portrait in his bedroom. He probably couldn't wait to get back to Zachary House and move it again—permanently. This time the painting would likely be consigned to the garbage heap.

After dinner the group returned to the mansion. The sun had not yet gone down in the summer-evening sky, and Caroline offered to show Cil the rose garden and the new pool that had been installed. As the two older women and Russell headed outside, Brian turned to Zana. "Well—" he gestured toward the stairs "—you've successfully made your way into my bedroom."

She smiled sweetly. "*I'm* not in your bedroom."

"Too bad. You'd be quite welcome there."

"That's not the impression I got last week. I was warned off quite emphatically."

"On the contrary. I was simply cautioning you not to have marriage on your mind. But bed..." He grinned, transforming his stern expression into something much more appealing. "I can see it now—that long silky hair streaming across my pillow."

"With Grandmother Zana monitoring everything we do?"

He laughed. "Granny definitely has to go."

"I figured you'd say that." Disconcerted, she tried to fabricate an air of indifference. She began checking out the rooms adjoining the foyer.

She simply didn't know what to make of Brian. Turning back, she saw that he was watching her, but this time his expression was clearly readable. He wanted her. The dramatic change troubled her even more. She wasn't comfortable engaging in sexual banter with Brian, and she didn't want to see any more of those suggestive looks. "Are you ready to accept our parents' marriage yet?" she asked, hoping to cool down the too-warm atmosphere.

Brian's face became an angry mask once more as he said, "What makes you ask that?" He glanced at the trio walking in the garden, then back at her. "I believe I made it perfectly clear. I'll not allow anyone to hurt Mother."

"Perhaps you haven't noticed, but she's quite capable of taking care of herself. Caroline's not some weak—"

"Weak? Mother? Of course not. If that's the conclusion you've drawn, then you haven't been listening very well. My mother had to work hard after my father's death. A lot of women wouldn't have made it. What I keep telling you is that I won't allow her to be hurt. A person doesn't have to be weak to have his heart broken."

Not *her* heart broken. Zana wondered if he was talking about himself, but she wasn't about to try to find out. "You didn't say anything about it this evening, so I...I supposed, uh, you'd accepted their marriage just as I have."

Brian slowly shook his head. "To tell the truth, I'm having a difficult time knowing what to do." He sighed. "My mother seems happier than she has in years. I don't want to spoil that happiness. I just don't want anyone else spoiling it, either."

"Like my father, you mean? Papa adores her. Any idiot can see that."

"Even me?"

"I wasn't trying to be insulting." She rubbed her hands together nervously. "Can't you just give them a little time?"

"I thought that was what I was doing. I'm not an ogre . . . am I?" His earnest expression went straight to her heart, confusing Zana completely.

She was sure of only one thing—Brian Westbrook was dangerous. Especially to a woman like her who didn't know from one minute to the next where she stood with the man or how she felt about him.

"How would you like some coffee?" he asked.

Zana nodded.

"Follow me. We can sit in the kitchen. It's too hot to have coffee on the patio."

While Brian spooned coffee into a filter, Zana perched on a bar stool, observing his familiarity with the kitchen. "I'm surprised you haven't hired household staff yet."

"In due time," he said. "Mother and I have never had any around, except for a weekly cleaning woman the past couple of years. A house this large will change all that."

The coffee had just finished brewing when the others joined Zana and Brian in the kitchen, apparently lured there by the aroma.

"Just what we were talking about," Caroline said as she crossed to the china cabinet for cups and saucers. Everyone took a seat around the kitchen table while Caroline poured. In deference to Russell's and

Cil's taste, the coffee was Louisiana-style, strong and black, the others adding extra cream to lessen the bitterness.

Cil turned to Brian. "Have you given any more thought to my idea of an open house?"

Zana watched as Brian began to look trapped again. "Yes. There's some merit to your suggestion," he said diplomatically, "but I'm too involved with the renovations and relocating my company to even think about one. Why don't you and Mother work out a date and I'll turn the planning over to the two of you?"

"Wonderful!" they said in unison.

Brian cast a quick glance Zana's way, and she could tell he was patting himself on the back for agreeing to the older women's suggestion without being forced to handle the preparations. She didn't have the heart to tell him that he'd only won a temporary reprieve. She knew Aunt Cil, and Caroline seemed to be her kindred spirit. Before he could say major migraine, those two women would have him immersed up to his earlobes in party details.

After coffee the group went to the front door for goodbyes. Zana was the last to leave, and as she was bidding Brian good-night, he held her back so that the two of them were left alone on the porch. "See you later," he said softly, and bent his head toward hers.

Zana wasn't sure what she expected, but what she got was another one of those awful platonic kisses on the cheek. Was he deliberately taunting her? For the umpteenth time, she struggled with her conflicting emotions as she descended the front steps. *Be grateful he's not putting more moves on you,* she told herself.

And yet, she couldn't stop comparing the two kisses she'd gotten today with the one they'd shared when he'd first brought her to Zachary House. She shook her head in disgust. *What's wrong with me, anyway?*

"WELL, I'M GLAD that's over," Russell said as he plopped down into his easy chair in the living room.

"Was it so bad, dear? Being with Brian?" Caroline sat on the arm of his chair and gently stroked his forehead.

"No, no," he said. "Actually our visit was quite pleasant. I just worried so much about what might happen when we spent some time together that I couldn't quite relax around him." He smiled at Caroline. "Obviously I've worried for nothing. So I promise to banish all such thoughts from my mind." He slipped an arm around his wife's waist.

"I'm sorry Brian came on so strong at first," Caroline said sympathetically. "His father died young, and Brian was forced to take on a lot of responsibility. Now he thinks he's in charge of everything—including my life."

Caroline smiled at Zana and Lucille. "My son will just have to learn to let me live my own life." As her own words sunk in, Caroline gave a soft laugh. "Sounds funny, doesn't it, for a parent to be saying such a thing. Usually it's the child complaining. I guess that somewhere along the way our roles got switched."

Zana listened with interest. She remembered recently thinking the same thing about herself and Russell. She was still mulling over the conversation an hour later when everyone else was in bed and she was checking the locks and turning out the lights before retiring herself. It seemed that her days of taking care of Russell were over. She also realized that it was time to make a decision about her own future. Her father had moved on; it was time for her to do the same. Perhaps she'd better call Kurt and find out if his offer was still open.

She slept fitfully, waking often to the sound of a soft breeze fluttering the leaves of the pecan tree outside her window. When morning arrived, she was almost as tired as when she'd gone to bed, and also totally unprepared for the day's activities as prescribed by her dynamic housemates.

Caroline handed her a glass of grapefruit juice as soon as she appeared in the kitchen. "Drink up, dear. We're in a rush."

"So many things to do," Cil joined in. "And simply no time. Since the furnishings will be in place before the end of the week, we've planned the festivities sometime within the next month. And instead of an open house, a gala. A ball."

"A Saturday night would be best, don't you think?" Caroline's question was directed to Zana.

Zana nodded and finished her juice. What she thought hardly mattered, she knew. These two had turned into a party-planning machine, and heaven help anyone who got in its way. Making herself as scarce as possible over the next few weeks would be the smartest thing to do.

But the women weren't about to let her be uninvolved. "We want to look through the attic this morning—you'll enjoy that dear." Cil patted her cheek. "There are boxes and trunks—a real treasure trove. It'll be a costume ball, of course. 'Zachary House, from Past to Present'—that's what we'll put on the invitations. Then if anyone wants to be obstinate about wearing a costume, they can still come. Maybe we can find outfits for ourselves. One of the trunks is packed with old clothes. Now, hurry your father along, dear. I can't wait to get to that attic."

MUCH TO ZANA'S RELIEF, Brian was nowhere around when the group arrived at Zachary House. Not that there was any time for visiting with him. Briskly reminding them of their task, Caroline ushered everyone upstairs to the attic where Cil and Russell opened one trunk after another, happily uncovering long-lost family treasures and sharing the story of each one.

Lucille took an old sepia print out of a box. "Oh, look, Zana! This is your grandmother's wedding photo." It was a full-length shot of Zana Davis on the day that she'd married Edmund Zachary. She wore a dress of white satin and lace, high-necked and wasp-waisted, with long puffed sleeves.

Zana was utterly taken with the elegance of the dress and the natural beauty of the bride. "I'd love to look like this on my wedding day," she said. "If I ever get married, that is."

"You will, dear, you will," Lucille stated. "And maybe sooner than you think."

Zana glanced at her aunt in surprise, then remembered who was speaking. Her beloved Aunt Cil considered hyperbole and sweeping generalizations necessary to all conversations. Zana was saved from having to respond to Lucille's prediction, though, because Russell distracted the group with a stack of old Confederate bills he'd laughingly pulled from a trunk.

Despite her relief that Brian was nowhere to be seen, Zana couldn't stop thinking about him. Was he still asleep, nestled in that big soft bed? Was he wearing anything? Zana started to blush, and self-consciously she glanced over at the others, but they were still blissfully rooting through boxes, completely unaware of her.

She tried to switch her thoughts from Brian to ballet, but merely succeeded in making things worse. She could only seem to remember the pas de deux from *Sleeping Beauty*. She shook her head trying to clear the images from her mind. Better to concentrate on the trip to the past with the others.

A few hours later her companions had taken a break and gone out for hamburgers. Zana had remained in the attic, too fascinated by her discoveries to bother eating. Obituaries, wedding invitations and dance cards from pre-Civil War balls filled trunk after trunk. She'd even found a young girl's diary with a rose pressed between its pages. She'd just pulled an ivory Christening dress from a nest of yellowed tissue paper when Brian came into the attic, ducking to avoid hitting his head on the low frame of the entryway.

"Ah, babies. Do you want children, Zana?"

She could have answered him with a simple yes. She'd always planned to have a family. Sometime. But with Brian, no answer was simple. She was certain his question was not at all innocent. "That's none of your concern," she said finally.

"Surely you're not depending on our parents to further the Zachary line?" He crossed the room and seated himself on the floor close to her, too close, Zana thought.

Avoiding eye contact, she busied herself with folding the tiny garment. "It's too early in the day for barbs. Besides, I've been instructed by your party committee to find costumes for the ball."

"Ball? What happened to the open house? I should have known better than to turn those two loose." He shook his head. "So what are you doing with this?" He lifted the baby's dress from her hands. "It won't fit anyone I know."

"I got sidetracked when I saw it, which wasn't hard to do. There's so much here." Zana gestured around the room. There were at least six trunks not yet opened. "I can't imagine it all still being around."

"I was amazed to discover a full attic," Brian admitted. "My new home seems to be a warehouse for Zachary memorabilia."

Zana didn't know what kind of response to make. She sat staring down at her hands until Brian lifted her chin. "Don't act so forlorn. I . . ."

She looked at him expectantly. But he didn't continue. What had he started to say? What had stopped him? For a moment she felt certain he was going to kiss her. She *wanted* him to kiss her, but he didn't. The silence became unbearable.

"Why do you toy with me like that?" she said at last.

"Like what?"

"You know what I'm talking about."

Brian rose from his place on the floor, then deliberately dusted off the back of his jeans and sat on top of a closed trunk. "Maybe it's the desperate act of a man who's fallen in love."

Zana scoffed. "Now you're insulting my intelligence. You've been very emphatic in expressing your opinions about the fallacy of love. So why try to bait me? Especially after all the remarks you made about being my brother."

"I'm definitely not your brother."

"I vividly recall you calling yourself that."

Brian shrugged. "That was a long time ago." Suddenly he stood and lifted Zana from the floor, giving her no time to react. Instead, he covered her lips with his, surprising her with a passionate kiss. He held her tightly, and Zana pressed herself against the contours of his muscular chest. She tried to think, to convince herself she was making a mistake, but she couldn't prevent her body from responding.

As their lips parted and they looked into one another's eyes, he touched her cheek with his fingertips before moving his hand to her neck and urging her close again.

This kiss was even more demanding than the first. She could feel the rapid beat of his heart and knew it was matched by her own. Waves of desire began to ripple through her body and her only thought was a wish for more.

When Brian released her for the second time, she reached for him in an attempt to steady herself. He, too, seemed shaken, and Zana doubted that their embrace would have ended if they hadn't heard car doors slamming in the distance, signaling the return of Aunt Cil and their parents.

CHAPTER SIX

"But I bought it for *you*." The sound of Brian's agitated voice awakened Zana. She glanced at the clock beside her bed. It was after ten—time to get up. She desperately needed a bit of caffeine, but didn't relish the idea of wandering into the kitchen for morning coffee and landing in the middle of a family squabble.

She cracked open the door of her bedroom and heard Caroline's more subdued voice. "I love to visit Zachary House, and I'm delighted that Russell can go there whenever he wishes, but neither of us wants to live off you."

"That's absurd."

"No, dear," Caroline chided. "That's exactly what you thought when Russell married me—that his motivation was greed. How can you possibly expect him to live in your house after everything you've said?"

Zana slipped on a robe and moved quietly down the hall. It wasn't polite to eavesdrop, but she couldn't resist. Anyway, Caroline knew she was in the house. Brian probably did, too. If they didn't care about her overhearing their conversation, why should she? Cil had returned to New Orleans yesterday, but where was Papa? Through the open kitchen door, she could see only two sitting at the table.

"I'm sorry if I've made you unhappy, Mother. That was the last thing I wanted to do."

"You were just operating true to form, Brian." Caroline laughed and patted his face to soften the gibe. "And you've been terribly unfair to Russell. When are you going to realize everyone isn't a gold digger like Claudette?" She shook her head. "I swear, every time I think about that conniving female, I want to chew nails. She's ruined your faith in people. I didn't like her when you were dating in high school, didn't like her when you were in college, and I most certainly didn't like her when she dumped you for that rich fraternity boy. But she keeps turning up like a bad penny. Now that she's divorced, she's after you again. When it comes to chasing men with money, that woman is tireless."

"Mother, we agreed not to talk about Claudette, remember?"

"You ordered. I didn't agree."

"I thought we were discussing the house, not my love life."

"Love? Don't make me laugh. Sex life is more like it. Oh, don't look so shocked. Sometimes you act as if I'm too old to even remember the word 'sex.'"

"Mother, drop this subject—please."

"Okay, I promise not to say the S-word again. You look as embarrassed about it now as you did when you were fourteen."

The next few words were muffled by water running in the sink, then Caroline's voice was intelligible once more. "About Claudette..."

"I don't want to talk about Claudette." Zana smiled at the irritated note in Brian's voice. His mother was obviously driving him to distraction. Yet despite her amusement, Zana didn't blame him for being exasperated with Caroline. Children of any age seldom appreciated a parent's interference.

"Good, we won't mention her again," Caroline said, then immediately proceeded to do so. "But I'll tell you one more thing—that red-haired hussy doesn't know the first thing about love. Unfortunately neither do you. I wish you would fall in love, Brian. It's wonderful."

"About the house?" Brian prodded impatiently.

"About Claudette," his mother countered. Zana realized where Brian had gotten his obstinacy. Mother and son were two of a kind.

"Oh, for Pete's sake, Mother. I haven't seen Claudette in over a month. I doubt I'll be seeing her again. So can we please get back to discussing the house? The alterations in the east wing will give you and Russell plenty of privacy."

"Most of the time I overlook your obtuseness and excuse it by saying you're too involved in your computers. But I'm coming to the conclusion that you only hear what you want to hear. For the last time, Brian, Russell and I are *not* moving to Zachary House."

"But I bought it for you. It's your dream house."

"You bought it for yourself, dear," Caroline said matter-of-factly. "It was your dream, not mine. A fancy home has never been important to me. I've found my little piece of heaven right here."

Brian snorted. "This place?"

"It's a lot better than most of the homes I've had. Besides, when and if you ever do fall in love, you'll discover that where you're living is secondary to whom you're living with."

"So what do I do with the house?"

"Live there, and in the meantime, try to find yourself a nice girl to marry. Then present me with a couple of grandchildren and my happiness will be complete."

Zana moved closer to the kitchen and glimpsed Caroline rising from her chair and patting her son's shoulder. "Now, while I finish making coffee, you pop some bread into the toaster and call Zana for breakfast. I just heard the car. Russell's back with the milk."

Zana rushed down the hall and into the bathroom before Brian could catch her eavesdropping. She'd jump into the shower, then join everyone for the morning meal.

Humming a tune from *The Nutcracker Suite* while she showered, Zana tried to ignore the realization that her good humor was the result of learning Brian wasn't still seeing his college sweetheart.

When she appeared in the kitchen, she sensed that Russell's return had ended all discussion of moving into Zachary House. He and Brian were reading different sections of the morning paper and Caroline was putting cereal bowls on the place mats. However, the four of them had barely begun to eat when Brian brought up the topic again. "Mr. Zachary—"

"Brian," Russell interrupted, "why don't you call me Russell. There's no need to be so formal."

"Russell," Brian began anew, "Mother tells me you've chosen not to live at the estate. I want you to know you're quite welcome there."

"I appreciate that." Russell reached for a packet of sweetener and tore open a corner. "I know you were concerned about our elopement, particularly about my intentions." He calmly poured the sweetener into his coffee, added some milk and stirred the mixture.

Zana watched in amazement. After witnessing her father's withdrawal for the past year, she'd never expected to see him this confident and self-possessed again.

"I've not had a lot of money," he went on, "but I've held my own, supported my family. Until the accident, that is. After that, Zana and I were forced to use all the insurance her mother had left, then dip into Zana's savings. Let me tell you, it wasn't an easy time for me."

Russell paused for a moment and took Caroline's hand. "When I first met your mother, Brian, I wouldn't have considered asking her to marry me— I just wasn't in any financial position to do so. But then there was a big change in my life. A change I haven't even shared with Zana. An unexpected windfall."

Zana looked at him skeptically. She was afraid of what was coming next. In the past her father had made some very foolish investments—in the stock market just as it turned bearish, in a time-share condo in Switzerland that no one ever used, in a prize fighter who spent more time on his back than on his feet. Russell had no head for money and had always been too susceptible to sales pitches.

"You know the story of my disinheritance, Zana," Russell said. "I can't say there haven't been times in my life when I didn't regret my actions, didn't wish I'd reached some sort of compromise with my father. But then, he wasn't what you would call a compromising man and I was young and impetuous.

"It took a few years, but eventually I met Vivi," he squeezed Caroline's hand, "and then Zana came along... Well, Zachary House and the business couldn't compare to life with the two of them. Besides, most of the old existence was gone for me. My mother had died when I was a teenager, and I never heard from my father again after our last argument. Cil stayed in contact, but Dad made it very clear he wanted nothing more to do with me. On his orders, my name was not mentioned in Zachary House.

"So no one was more surprised than I when a lawyer contacted me on the Friday you went to Jackson. Unknown to Cil or me, my father had arranged a trust—a trust I would receive only if I returned to Natchez on my own and stayed here for at least six months. It's not a lot of money, but it'll keep Caroline and me in comfort for the rest of our days. If I'd never returned, eventually it would have gone to charity. My father was going to have his way, even in death."

Zana mentally calculated—they'd been in Natchez for about seven months.

"I guess I got a little crazy after meeting with that young lawyer," Russell continued. "I had the urge to go home, home to Zachary House. Caroline happened to be there when I arrived and, well, one thing led to another. I'm not sure exactly when we decided to get married. But you were in Jackson, honey, and Brian—'' his gaze went from Zana to Brian ''—you were off in Europe.''

''But why did you get married so quickly?'' Zana asked.

''Why not?'' her father answered. ''At our age time is a luxury not to be wasted.''

''Besides, we wanted to be together,'' Caroline added. ''We were lonely. You both feel responsible for us and try to take care of us, but that's not enough.''

It was obvious to Zana that her father no longer depended on her. Zana wasn't sure whether to feel relieved or hurt. But her feelings didn't really matter, not when he was this happy.

She glanced at Brian. He seemed to be going through some of the same mental machinations as she, his face registering confusion and frustration.

''I'll have to admit most of my concerns have been laid to rest,'' Brian said, ''but we still haven't resolved the issue of Zachary House. Why don't you two move over there for a while and see how you like it? As you've pointed out, I'm gone a great deal. You'd have plenty of privacy.''

''I just don't know, dear,'' Caroline clasped her hands together and demurely placed them on the table. ''We're content here. We've never considered living at Zachary House. It's too big.''

"How come it's too big for three, but it wasn't too big for the two of us?" her son asked.

"Things are quite different now. And don't forget, we have to think about Zana."

"Yes," Russell interjected. "We can't desert Zana."

Brian looked exasperated. "Naturally Zana's welcome, too. There's plenty of room for everyone."

Zana was annoyed at the others for talking about her as if she was a dotty relative who needed a keeper. "Don't worry about me," she said, trying not to let her irritation show. "I may not even stay in Natchez. Kurt Rutherford offered me a job in London, and I'm seriously thinking about accepting."

All eyes turned to her.

"Baby, that's wonderful!" Russell leaned over to wrap an arm around her shoulder. "London. When I think of the good times we had there. What a grand city. And just a short hop from Paris and Rome."

"Is this a rational decision or has wanderlust taken hold again?" Brian asked curtly. His question was directed at Zana, but his gaze was on her father. It was a none-too-subtle warning that Russell Zachary had better not get any ideas about packing his suitcases.

She should have known Brian would twist her father's words. Now that he no longer had money as an excuse to condemn Russell, he had to find another tack. If only Papa didn't sound so enthusiastic about the offer, she thought. Frankly, she was surprised he was, for she'd half expected him to caution her against working for Kurt. Although he hadn't been openly negative about her partner, Russell had never seemed particularly fond of Kurt. Could it be that Russell was anxious to spend some time alone with his new wife? Was Zana getting in the way?

She had been agonizing over her choices, but perhaps the decision had been taken out of her hands. Once again, her father's actions might dictate her own future.

Regardless of where Caroline and Russell lived, was there a place for her in Natchez? If the couple stayed in the small rental house, then she'd be underfoot. If they moved to Zachary House, then what? Would they insist she go along? She had no intention of living under Brian Westbrook's roof. And it wouldn't be practical to keep this house for just herself. No, the best solution would be for her to take the position Kurt had offered, and try to forget stubborn men with soft Southern drawls and attitude problems. But why did the idea make her feel so miserable?

For the next week the proposed ball seemed forgotten, instead the issue of where Russell and Caroline would live monopolized all family discussions. Brian continued to insist they move into Zachary House; Russell and Caroline continued to refuse.

Zana felt stuck between two unyielding forces, especially since every time Brian brought up the subject, Caroline countered with her what-about-Zana argument. It was obvious that Caroline had recognized Zana's wish to keep her distance from Brian and was using the knowledge to her own advantage.

Finally Zana decided to take matters in hand. She called Kurt.

"Of course there's still a job for you," he assured her. "And even if the post had been filled, I'd always find a spot for my favorite partner."

Zana felt no elation when she hung up the phone. Kurt had been a little too happy to hear from her. She recalled Brian's assertion that Kurt was in love with her. Much as she hated to admit it, Brian was probably right. And if it was true, then it was unfair of her to raise Kurt's hopes. Besides, she hadn't forgotten how difficult Kurt could be when he didn't get his way. Maybe working in London wasn't the answer. But what other choice did she have?

The next evening, while her father was napping, Zana decided to tell Caroline she'd called Kurt. She'd fretted over what to do long enough. It was time to let her family know what she'd decided.

Zana was unprepared for the tears that welled up in her stepmother's eyes. "I feel so guilty. This is all my fault. What is your father going to say?"

"Papa thought it was a good idea."

"No, no. He *hates* it. But he feels awful for forcing you to come back to Mississippi. He thinks you're excited by the chance to leave. I think he's wrong. You don't really want to leave, do you? You're just going away because of me." Caroline began weeping in earnest.

Zana didn't know what to do or say. She found herself hugging the older woman and begging her not to blame herself. "My decision had nothing to do with you," she fibbed. "I just want to be more involved in ballet."

Caroline stopped crying but she continued to berate herself as she wandered around the kitchen, hunting for a pot holder and removing a pan of zucchini muffins from the oven.

Hoping to ease her conscience, Zana readily agreed when Caroline asked her to stop by Zachary House with some muffins for Brian. "I was planning to deliver them myself, but if I go, he'll see my puffy eyes and start asking questions," Caroline said.

Zana would have been willing to do anything to get away from Caroline's self-recrimination. She was halfway to the mansion before it dawned on her that she'd been taken in. How many times had she been sent there lately, anyway? If Brian wasn't being invited to dinner, then Zana was being sent to Zachary House on one errand or another. Caroline was obviously using every opportunity to throw Brian and Zana together. The notion was surprising, not to mention unsettling. What would Brian think about his mother's attempts at matchmaking?

Zana knew the answer—he'd be furious. And if he already was aware of Caroline's efforts, he'd be relieved to hear of Zana's decision to go to London.

Brian, however, didn't respond as anticipated. "What are you trying to achieve by doing this?" He met her at the car, his lips pressed together in an angry grimace. "Mother called and told me about your conversation. I thought when you mentioned Kurt the other night, you were being perverse. I never dreamed you really meant it."

Brian's words confirmed Zana's suspicions that she'd been set up. Caroline had decided not to argue with her; instead, she'd turned the battle over to a more able warrior. He took the plate of muffins from Zana and set it on the hood of the car, then grabbed her upper arm. "Why are you creating problems for everyone?"

She backed up against the car, futilely trying to put some space between them. "I'm trying to solve a problem, not create one. Now let me go." She jerked her arm but Brian's grip held.

"Is that how you see it? You'll make everyone happy by jumping up and leaving? Don't you realize how much that distresses my mother? She feels like she's chased you away from your own home. Can't you put up with the situation for just a while longer, to make her—them—happy?''

"Them?''

"Your father, too, of course. Russell's even more miserable than Mother. And when he's unhappy, that upsets her.''

"I believe you're the one who told me to quit protecting my father. I'm simply trying to follow your advice,'' she said, removing his fingers from her arm.

"Well, that's a first. Since you're listening, here's something else to think about—you've been catering to Russell all your life, so why can't you continue doing that for another few months? Give them some time to get settled into their marriage. Besides, he's worried about your working with Rutherford. He's never liked the guy, you know.''

Zana couldn't recall Russell ever actually saying a bad word about Kurt, or anyone else for that matter. Even the criticisms he'd had of his own father had been mild. "I don't believe you,'' she said.

"Ask him, then. He'll tell you how he's fretted about that pointy-toed Lothario.''

Zana chewed her lower lip. Had Russell been concerned enough to actually discuss the subject with Brian?

"Well, then, Mr. Westbrook, if I don't go to London, what do I do? Things can't continue as they are. Most of the time I feel like a voyeur in my home. Our parents need to be alone. I can stay in Natchez and get an apartment, but what will that accomplish? Your mother will still feel guilty about pushing me out. You see, I'm at an impasse. So, what do *you* suggest?

"I don't know," he admitted. "But I'll think of something." He gave her a challenging look. "Or maybe together we can come up with a solution. Have dinner with me tonight and we'll talk about it."

"We can talk about it now. If you have any ideas, out with them."

Brian glanced at his watch. "I'm supposed to see a client within the hour, and I can see you're going to the studio. Tonight's soon enough. I'll pick you up at seven."

"WEAR YOUR RED SUNDRESS, dear. The one with the matching cardigan. Brian prefers bright colors." Caroline was hovering at the door of Zana's bedroom issuing instructions like a stage mother on opening night, and Zana was having second thoughts about the wisdom of letting Brian pick her up. It would have been better to meet him somewhere and not let their parents know about it.

Russell wasn't any subtler than Caroline. He'd been in and out of Zana's room half a dozen times, telling her the bathroom was free, asking if she needed anything pressed, suggesting she wear her hair loose. Zana felt like a sacrificial lamb.

Did Caroline and her father think there was something going on between her and Brian? As if Aunt Cil's innuendos weren't enough to deal with. Well, the three would-be Cupids could just look for other victims. Brian Westbrook didn't believe in love or marriage, and Zana wasn't about to be anyone's plaything.

Still, she welcomed the sight of him, welcomed being with him. She told herself she'd merely wanted to escape her interfering relatives, that those tingly feelings had nothing to do with Brian. Yet, half an hour later, as they made their way across the restaurant to a table overlooking the Mississippi, she couldn't help but be satisfied by the admiring glances other women gave him.

He was probably the best-looking man she'd ever met, certainly the best-looking she'd ever gone out with. Not that this was a real date she reminded herself. They were simply meeting for dinner to discuss a problem. Still, any woman would enjoy having Brian for an escort. Especially when he was being charming, as he was tonight. He was witty and gracious, as well as careful to avoid any upsetting topics—almost too careful. Which made Zana very suspicious.

At first their conversation was mundane and neutral—the weather, classical music, a new mystery novel by a native Mississippian. The chardonnay Brian ordered with dinner, combined with the pleasant chitchat, helped her relax. She was almost surprised when he finally brought up the topic of Zachary House.

"I think I've hit upon a solution to the house problem. A solution that will satisfy both our parents."

"Oh?" Zana fingered the stem of her wineglass as she waited for Brian to continue.

"I'm convinced they're happy where they are and are planning to stay."

"What makes you so sure?"

"Mainly the fact that Russell bought the place from the rental company. You knew that, didn't you?"

Zana didn't. She gave a face-saving nod, not willing to admit to Brian that this was the first she'd heard about it. How like Russell not to tell her. He'd seldom informed her of any of his rash business deals until after the fact. She could only hope he hadn't already blown his whole inheritance. Accompanying the worry was a stab of resentment that her father had shared the decision with Brian and not her. Was he afraid to let her know? Afraid that the news would send her off to London?

"So that leaves me all alone in Zachary House." He reached across the table and took her hand, his touch startling her. "And where does it leave you, Zana? You've said you don't want to stay with the newlyweds."

"That's right. But I keep telling everyone I have a place to go—London."

"That's unacceptable. Besides, it's not what you really want, especially if it means being close to Rutherford again. He's desired you for years. Do you think he's going to stop once he's your boss? Not likely."

"I know that. But I'm a big girl—I can handle him. It's just that since the accident, my choices are limited. If I want to stay in ballet, it might be my only option."

"You can continue to teach here in Mississippi. If you want to be more involved, the people with the International Competitions in Jackson would probably be thrilled to hear from you."

"What if I want to perform?"

"Could you?" He looked skeptical but his tone was sympathetic.

"Maybe." Of course, even if she was able to perform, the question of whether she really wanted to dance remained. "So I stay. I still wouldn't be happy living with our parents." She shrugged. "And as I said earlier, I don't think moving to an apartment is the answer."

"Neither do I. Poor Zana." The twinkle in his eyes belied the words. "I'm afraid there's only one choice left. Come live with me in Zachary House. That will make everyone happy—except Kurt, of course."

Zana was speechless. "Live with *you?*" she sputtered, waiting for the rest of the joke. But his expression told her he was serious.

"Poor Zana?" she repeated. "You feel sorry for me so you've decided to allow me to impose on you?" She ground her teeth. "Well, no thanks. I don't want your pity and I don't want to live with you. Besides, what would Papa and Caroline say? I don't think living together is what those two have in mind for us."

"Maybe not. My mother's been dropping a lot of hints about how she wants grandchildren, and I'm sure the two of them would welcome a marriage between us. But we can convince them that's not going to happen."

"You've got this all figured out, haven't you? And just to keep your mother happy."

"Oh, I think we have to acknowledge how it'd please your father, too."

"I'm sick to death of your accusations about Papa. I think you're jealous of him."

"Jealous of Russell? Don't be ridiculous. I'm not the one unwilling to share my parent and threatening to run away. You've been the center of attention for so long you can't bear to let Mother in on the relationship."

"Did she say that?"

"Of course not." He signaled for the waiter and reached for his wallet. "Let's get out of here. I didn't anticipate an argument."

"I'm sure you thought I'd just meekly go along with your scheme."

"No. But I should have realized you'd be stubborn about this. You asked me to come up with a way to solve everybody's problems, and that's what I did. I figured you'd like the idea."

"Well, I don't. And I doubt Papa and Caroline will be enthusiastic about it, either. They'll consider it living in sin." She realized she sounded terribly Victorian. But she also knew her father wouldn't be comfortable with such an arrangement. Besides, *she* wasn't comfortable with the arrangement.

"I haven't suggested anything sinful. It's a big house. You can move into the wing Mother was going to have. We'll hardly be tripping over each other."

"Papa and Caroline will never agree—"

"We're not in diapers. We don't need their permission. Anyway, *I* think they'll be pleased by the solution."

Zana didn't know why he seemed intent on continuing the discussion once they'd started driving home. Surely Brian didn't want her living with him. She would have expected him to be relieved that she'd refused. "Not long ago you were warning me not to try to get you to the altar," she said. "No telling what you'll accuse me of if I agree to this."

Brian eased the car into her driveway and killed the headlights. "We'll drop the subject for now." He unbuckled his seat belt and leaned toward her. "All I ask is that you think about it, Zana. Okay?"

He was so close she could feel his breath on her cheek. She remembered their kisses, and she had to stop herself from reaching out to touch him.

"Okay?" he prompted.

"Okay, I'll think about it," she answered, her voice trembling with uncertainty. Her emotions and her attraction to Brian seemed to prevent her from being logical. How would their parents react? What would Aunt Cil say? She should be considering such practicalities. Instead, her thoughts were entirely on Brian, and how much she longed to be held by him, kissed by him....

CHAPTER SEVEN

THINK ABOUT IT, he'd said. Zana could do nothing else. After he'd brought her home she'd sought refuge from Caroline and Russell in the solitude of a bubble bath and tried to decide what to do.

Brian was right about the perils of working with Kurt. Besides, Kurt's romantic advances weren't the only problem; her heart wasn't really in ballet anymore. The desire to dance to the exclusion of all else was gone.

And Kurt would never be able to accept that. It didn't matter if she was performing or teaching, he'd expect her to put ballet first—before friends, before family, even before him. He'd want her priorities to reflect his own. Zana could just imagine the arguments they'd have.

She slept fitfully, twisting the covers as she tossed and turned, and waking as confused as she'd been when she'd gone to bed. Working with Kurt was a poor solution, but living with Brian would be worse. He'd assured her that their relationship would be platonic, yet, Zana knew problems would still arise.

Because of her parents' impractical nature, Zana had always tried to use her common sense. And that common sense was telling her the attraction between her and Brian was too strong to resist.

The logical thing to do was rent an apartment and be on her own. But logic seemed to have vanished lately. Besides, how could she do that without upsetting Caroline and her father?

Although it was early—not yet seven—Zana decided to go to the studio. She had no classes scheduled, but a few hours of practice might take her mind off everything. If she hurried, she might even avoid Russell and Caroline, since they usually took a walk about this time. The house was quiet, so she figured they'd already gone. She'd get dressed, grab a quick cup of coffee and leave a note for them on the kitchen table.

However, her departure wasn't swift enough. When Zana entered the kitchen, Caroline was at the stove, turning pancakes, and Russell was behind her with his arms around her waist. Both were oblivious to Zana's presence. *My goodness,* she thought, *he's nibbling on her ear!* The image shocked her, and she backed out of the room, careful not to make any noise. Grabbing her purse and dance bag, she headed out the front door.

Should I have said something? What could I have said? "Pardon me for intruding, but I wanted a cup of coffee?'' Zana talked to herself all the way to the dance studio, frustrated by them and herself.

Yesterday she'd glimpsed a stolen kiss in the hall, and the day before that she'd actually seen Caroline pat her husband's rear. Why didn't they act their age? She knew she was being ridiculous. After all, Russell and Caroline *were* newlyweds. But she was forever catching them in moments of intimacy, and she couldn't help resenting them. Perhaps if more time had elapsed since her mother's death she'd feel differently.

She changed into her tights and leotard and started a series of warm-up exercises, her thoughts drifting back to the scene she'd witnessed. She admitted to herself she'd be uncomfortable no matter how long it had been since her mother's death. She knew Russell and Caroline were behaving just like any normal married couple. But she also knew that most grown children would be embarrassed by such a display— even if both parents were their own.

Still, moving in with Brian wasn't the answer. That would create more difficulties than it would solve. She'd be better off with Kurt. At least with him she'd know what to expect—and they wouldn't be sharing accommodations. Why, then, had going to London become so unappealing?

Zana had been at the studio for several hours, but she still hadn't made any decisions. Finally, in an attempt to stop thinking about her dilemma, she performed a demanding solo from *Firebird,* pretended she was auditioning for Balanchine and imagined she'd been picked to costar with Baryshnikov on a movie set in Russia. She even tried out a couple of Russian phrases learned while she'd competed in Moscow. *"Vot moy paspart. Ya nye znayu ruskikh razmyeraf."* Zana thought she'd said, "Here is my passport," and, "I don't know Russian sizes," but she wasn't sure.

Nothing helped. Her thoughts stubbornly remained on her father, and Caroline and Brian—and Brian's crazy suggestion. Eventually her knee began to throb, and she abandoned her exercises to do some paperwork.

Zana was sitting in her office writing checks, her leg propped up on an extra chair, when Brian appeared.

He brushed some strands of windblown hair off his forehead and frowned. "You should keep the door locked. It's not safe when you're in here all alone."

"That's true. No telling who might barge in."

"I'm beginning to think I'm acquiring a sarcastic roommate."

"You may be, but it won't be me."

He lifted Zana's leg so that he could sit down, then placed it across his thighs. "Not doing well today?" he asked as he began massaging her calf.

"It's bothering me a little," Zana admitted, surprised that he'd so easily assessed the situation.

"Do you feel like getting away? I've got a picnic lunch in the car. I thought we could drive up the Natchez Trace and find a place to eat."

Although she'd been there twice since moving to Mississippi, the offer sounded appealing. Zana loved the historic highway that followed the route taken by Indians and buffalo centuries ago. Portions of the original path were still accessible, and she'd walked along them, imagining she'd traveled back in time. Surrounded by ancient forest, the only sounds she'd heard were a few bird calls and the gurgle of a small stream.

However, Zana wasn't about to spend a day in such a secluded spot with Brian. She turned to him trying to think of a good reason to decline. "In this weather?" she eventually managed. "It must be ninety-five degrees outside, and the humidity's unbearable."

"So we'll go to plan B. A poolside picnic at Zachary House."

"I'm not hungry, and I've got a lot of work left to do." She gestured at the papers spread out in front of her.

"It'll keep. You said you'd think about living with me. How can you make a decision without looking at the place again? The furniture for the east wing was delivered this morning, so it's ready for occupancy." He removed her leg from his lap and placed it on the floor, then pulled her from her chair. "Come on." He held up his wrist, to show her his watch. "Eleven-thirty. Almost lunchtime."

They compromised by taking a quick drive along the Trace, before returning to Zachary House for the picnic. They swam before eating, Brian overriding Zana's objection that she didn't have a suit by directing her to the bathhouse, where there were extras recently purchased by Caroline.

The cool water washed away the combined grime from the workout and the drive and the muggy day, and a soak in the whirlpool eased the throbbing in Zana's knee. She felt like purring as the churning water soothed her aches and helped her relax.

By midafternoon only a few scraps of food remained on the patio table, but Brian and Zana were still lazing in their chairs, sipping iced tea, served just the way Zana loved it—with lemon and mint leaves. Brian had even put up an umbrella to shield her fair skin from the sun.

"Why all this solicitude?" she asked finally.

"I'm showing you what a considerate housemate I'd be," he replied as he moved his chair out of the shade.

Zana watched the sunlight glisten on his damp hair and thought about what he'd said, knowing that his actions were prompted only by a misguided desire to make his mother happy. She found that thought particularly annoying.

"Did you mention your idea to our parents?"

"Of course not. This is between the two of us. If you agree, then we'll tell them."

"They won't think it's a good idea."

"Too bad. We didn't think their elopement was such a hot idea, either. But like it or not, it seems to be working out. Mother's happy. Russell's happy. Now we just have to figure out how to keep them that way, without making ourselves miserable."

"Living together will do it?"

"It wouldn't do any harm. Come on, Zana, don't be difficult."

"I don't know..."

Brian rose from the chair. "I can see it's time to call in the heavy artillery. Let's go look at the east wing—maybe that'll convince you." He extended his hand to help her up, and without letting go, started toward the house.

The large bedroom had obviously been planned with a feminine occupant in mind. The walls were a soft canary yellow, and the dominant colors in the curtains and carpeting were yellow and blue. The furnishings were Victorian antiques—a four-poster bed with a crocheted bedspread, a grouping of Currier and Ives prints, a hand-molded fireplace mantel. Two arrangements of mixed flowers added a warm pleasant touch to the room.

"Caroline's choices are lovely," Zana said. "Too bad she won't be enjoying them firsthand."

"My sentiments exactly. That's another reason not to let all this go to waste. Her loss could be your gain."

"Well, I admit I'm tempted." She did love the room. She could see herself living here with only a couple of changes. A rocker by the fireplace and a pillow for the window seat would make the bedroom perfect. "No, it'll never work." She shook her head to emphasize her words. *What am I thinking of? I can't live with Brian.*

"Why not, for Pete's sake?" Brian reacted as if he'd heard her thoughts as well as her words. "Can't you at least consider it for a couple of months? That would solve our immediate problem. I'm sure Kurt will be willing to hold the . . . job that long."

"The job isn't the issue."

"Then why? And don't answer 'because.' I want a real reason."

"And you always get what you want." Zana wasn't up to discussing this any further. She was *too* tempted. By the room, and by the thought of living with Brian. "I'm sorry, but no."

"I won't take no for an answer. What harm will a few weeks do? We're not talking about a long-term lease. If you hate it, you can pack up and leave whenever you wish." Brian folded his arms across his chest and thrust his chin out stubbornly. "It's up to you. But frankly, I don't see why I have to listen to my mother weep just because you can't compromise."

Zana felt a moment of guilt. He was right—she was being too rigid. After all, if he was willing to put up with her living there, then surely she could handle the situation for a little while. They just needed to set a few ground rules. "What about rent?"

"Don't be ridiculous. I'm not going to charge you rent."

"I'd insist on some kind of payment. I absolutely refuse to live off you."

"Okay, we'll work it out, whatever you're comfortable with, so long as you say yes." Brian relaxed visibly and reached out to run his knuckles along her jawline.

Briefly Zana thought he was going to pull her into his arms—and for a moment she'd have willingly let him. She could feel his embrace, taste his kiss. However, that made her realize just how foolish moving into Zachary House would be. She'd tell him she'd changed her mind, and this time force him to accept her decision. But when she opened her mouth to tell him, she found herself agreeing instead.

"All right," she said, "we'll do it, but strictly on a trial basis."

"Agreed," he said, looking immensely pleased with himself.

"And one more thing," she added, trying to regain her composure. "If I live here, our relationship must be platonic. Am I making myself clear?"

His lips formed a wry smile. "No kissing?"

"No kissing. No leg massages. No touching. No *anything*. Okay?"

"Okay," he echoed, holding out his hand to seal the promise.

Zana's hands stayed clenched at her sides.

"I forgot, no touching." Brian's smile was wide now and entirely too self-satisfied.

She didn't care. He could think he'd achieved some sort of victory. The truth was, Zana herself felt surprisingly relieved. Moving out meant that she wouldn't be intruding on Russell and Caroline, and would also give her more time to make a final decision about her future. It was now late July, and Kurt had told her classes wouldn't start until fall. She could still join him then if she wanted. And if she didn't? Well, coming to Zachary House would make getting a place of her own that much easier.

"We might as well tell everyone then," she said. "Aunt Cil's coming up here this weekend to make arrangements for the ball, so we can talk to all three of them at once."

IT WAS DARK when Brian drove her back to the studio for her car. She'd called Russell and Caroline earlier to let them know where she was, and was relieved they didn't quiz her about her afternoon—or anything else—once she'd arrived.

They were too busy playing a duet on the piano and violin to pay much attention. Not that she really minded. Seeing how happy the two were together forced Zana to once again acknowledge that the marriage had been a blessing for them both.

She sat on the edge of her bed later that night, staring at her distorted image reflected in the darkened windows. She couldn't believe she'd actually agreed to move into Zachary House. Apparently, she wasn't capable of thinking straight in Brian's presence. Something about him confused her and led her to do things she regretted.

Through the thin walls, she heard Russell and Caroline preparing for bed, then the creak of the mattress and springs as they retired. Were they making love? No, she decided, she'd be able to hear that, too—which was another reason the cottage was too small for the three of them.

But how could she consider sharing a house with Brian when she fantasized about him in such inappropriate ways? She'd often yearned for a man to hold her and make love to her. In her imaginings the man had always been faceless—but not now. Now it was Brian.

Perhaps it was a mistake to move into Zachary House, but she knew she'd do it anyway. After all, she'd only be there for a little while. Just long enough to get Russell and Caroline settled, and her own life in order.

BRIAN INVITED EVERYONE to dinner at Zachary House on Saturday night. The meal was prepared by Maudie, the new cook, and served in the formal dining room. He'd told Zana he hoped the elegant setting would help the others see Zana's moving in as the only reasonable answer to their problems. When they saw her in the familiar surroundings, they'd realize it was the only logical place for her to be.

For most of the evening Cil and Caroline had prattled on about the ball, Cil insisting a date had to be set soon so invitations could be ordered. They'd just been served dessert—praline pound cake and coffee—when Brian cleared his throat. "Zana and I have an announcement to make."

All attention became focused on him. Aunt Cil had a forkful of cake halfway to her mouth, but returned it to her plate as she paused to hear him out.

"Zana's going to move into the east wing—the side that was originally intended for Mother—" he glanced quickly at Caroline "—which will make us housemates, so to speak."

For long moments, the only sound in the dining room was the soft whir of the ceiling fan.

Eventually Caroline broke the silence. "That's, uh, nice, dear," she said.

When no one else commented, Brian looked at Zana's aunt. "Cil? Are you speechless all of a sudden?"

"I guess I am. To tell the truth, I think I was expecting you to say something quite different."

Zana knew exactly what Cil, and the other two, had been expecting—a wedding announcement. They were all disappointed. Even Sid, who was lying on a sideboard beside the table, appeared to be looking at her with disapproval.

But Brian didn't seem to notice. "Well, now that that's settled, let's adjourn to the solarium for more coffee." The group quietly went into the inviting room and sat on the comfortable sofas and oversize wing chairs, where they spent the next hour exchanging meaningless pleasantries. Talk of the ball had waned, but it was obvious to Zana that everyone was purposely avoiding the topic of her move.

The next morning Zana began packing. Since she wouldn't be staying at Zachary House for long, she had to figure out what to do with the items she wouldn't need right away. If she left anything behind, she'd have to tell everyone of her plans, and she didn't want to do that. In the end, she put all her belongings into boxes, some of which she'd take to Zachary House, and the others she'd store at her studio.

The following day, Brian sent a van over, driven by his new grounds keeper who helped her load and transport all her boxes.

Brian was in Memphis overseeing his company's transfer, and Zana was glad to have the house to herself. She felt awkward enough as it was. Even though no one had said anything, she knew Russell, Caroline and Cil didn't approve of what was happening.

She smiled at the thought of Aunt Cil's uncharacteristic silence. It wasn't like her to remain quiet on any subject, but so far she had. Zana wouldn't have been surprised, though, to discover that her aunt had discussed the situation with Russell and Caroline before returning to New Orleans.

Brian may not have been around the day she moved in, but it was difficult avoiding him from then on. Even in the spacious house, with them living in separate wings, it seemed as if their paths were continually crossing. Once he was going out for a jog, and she was headed toward the kitchen when they bumped into each other in the hall. Brian stepped to the side with a cursory apology, then continued on his way. But Zana was so affected by the encounter that her hand was shaking several minutes later as she poured chicory-flavored coffee from the carafe.

Only a day or so later, Brian was carrying a new table to the second floor at the exact moment she was leaving for work. He made an elaborate show of pressing himself against the table to give her room to pass, but despite leaning back over the banister, she still brushed against him.

Then late one night, they both appeared in the kitchen to get something to drink. Zana had come down dressed in only an oversize T-shirt, expecting to be alone. So, she was embarrassed when Brian flipped on the kitchen light and saw her at the refrigerator. "Uh, I'm just here for milk," she mumbled, and quickly poured a glass before bolting for the door.

She was becoming convinced these meetings weren't accidental. She was sure Brian was mocking her and the agreement they'd made. He wasn't even allowing her to pay rent, at least not really. She had determined the cost of the most luxurious accommodation in the area. That unit paled in comparison to her rooms at Zachary House, and didn't offer maid service or any of the amenities she enjoyed. But it was the only measuring stick she had, so she wrote Brian a check for the same amount.

When she'd given him the check, he'd tucked it into his shirt pocket—where for all she knew it still remained. It hadn't been cashed, and she suspected he had no intention of ever cashing it. The thought angered her; she didn't want to be indebted to Brian Westbrook.

Zana was backing down the stairs, trying to dislodge the rocker she had taken from the attic. It had become stuck in the curve of the stairs. She gave another pull, letting out a squeal of surprise when she bumped into something solid. It was Brian standing behind her on the steps. "We've got to stop meeting like this," he said, pressing against her as he maneuvered around her to grab the chair.

"I don't need your help," she protested, disturbed by the contact of their bodies.

"Be sensible. The rocker's bigger than you are." Because she hadn't yet let go, his arms were intertwined with hers. In an effort to avoid his touch, she accidentally pushed the chair, wedging it more.

She glared at him. "Now look what you've done. Why won't you leave me alone. I'm fed up with your games." Zana knew she was overreacting, but he was so close she could hardly breathe. She had to have some space.

Brian released his hold on the chair and propped his hands against the wall over her head. They were no longer touching, but she was now caught between him and the rocker.

"I'm not sure what you're talking about, but I can tell you, I'm not playing any games." His expression was serious. "This arrangement is more difficult than I thought it would be."

Perhaps she'd misjudged him. Perhaps she'd subconsciously caused some of their other encounters and was blaming them all on him.

"You're right," she said, sitting down on a stair. Brian lowered himself beside her. "The problem is that our situation is unnatural. I'm sure you're used to... used to social engagements." Brian hadn't invited a woman into the house since she'd moved in. His only guests had been a couple of buddies who'd come over to watch a preseason football game. "I'm not comfortable asking anyone in, either. It's not normal. We should both be dating."

"Dating?" he said contemptuously. "You want to *date?*" He made it sound as if she'd suggested allowing a battalion of men to stay in the east wing. Why was he so hostile? All she'd wanted was to ease the awkwardness of their situation.

"Well, uh, yes. Most single people our age do date."

"Anyone in particular—or is Kurt coming back to grace us with his presence?"

"Is there some other reason for this snit," she snapped, "besides jealousy?"

"I'm not—" He paused, then grinned guiltily. "I'm tired and hungry. Maybe that's my excuse."

"It's Maudie's day off. Why don't you let me earn my keep by preparing something to eat?"

"Nah, let's go out for a hamburger."

"Thanks, but unlike you, I'm not really hungry."

"So come and keep me company then."

When she didn't answer he smiled boyishly and added, "Please?"

"Oh, all right. If you'll take this chair to my room, I'll grab my purse." She wasn't sure if Brian's anger had totally disappeared, but maybe this would be a good time to convince him that she should move.

They drove to a fast-food place and eased into a shiny plastic booth where they ate, surrounded by the din of chattering kids and the frequent announcements of orders over the loudspeaker. Zana had given in to the lure of food and ordered a hamburger and a vanilla shake.

Soon she was relaxed and laughing. Brian was at his most witty and entertaining. She couldn't help giggling at the tale of his receptionist, Pauline, discovering a mouse in the file cabinet during their packing. Apparently Dennis, one of his programmers who was about six foot four and well over two hundred pounds, had a morbid fear of rodents and ended up crouching on top of a desk while Pauline chased the mouse around the office with a broom.

They'd stayed at the restaurant for more than an hour and it turned out to be quite a different experience from what Zana had anticipated. Their parents, Zachary House and her wish to move had never even entered the conversation.

When they returned home, Brian parked the car and reached for her hand. "I don't want you to leave, Zana." Then without another word, she was in his arms and his lips were against hers. He was kissing her senseless, and she didn't care.

He finally broke the kiss and got out of the car, then came around to the passenger side to help her out. When she emerged from the Jaguar, he pulled her to him again, and by the time this second kiss ended, her legs were threatening to buckle under her. Brian must have known how unsteady she was, because he picked her up and carried her into the house.

Once inside, he gently removed his arm from under her legs, causing her to slide down his body until her feet touched the floor. Then he trapped her between his body and the foyer door and kissed her a third time, slowly, his lips tantalizingly soft at first, then deeply demanding. All too soon, though, he released her.

"There's passion between us, passion neither of us can ignore," he said, before turning on his heel and heading up the stairs, leaving Zana grasping the doorknob for support.

CHAPTER EIGHT

IN THE FOLLOWING WEEK, Brian said nothing further about their living arrangements, and he cut off any attempt of Zana's to tell him she was moving. She'd even located a place—a one-bedroom apartment in a small complex near the studio.

Not that she and Brian had many opportunities to talk—their hectic schedules saw to that. But Zana found this preferable to their awkward meetings, because she was still unsettled by the kisses they'd shared. And she was glad she'd only agreed to stay at Zachary House for a trial period and could leave at any time without recriminations.

Brian, however, changed her plans. She was having a sandwich in the kitchen one night, watching the small-screen TV, when he ambled in. He'd been upstairs all evening and this was the first time she'd seen him, although she'd heard him return home hours ago. He grabbed a can of soda from the refrigerator and joined her at the table. She turned off the television.

"This living arrangement isn't going to work." He paused to take a drink.

Zana was surprised and relieved. Apparently she and Brian were sharing the same sentiments, and he was getting ready to ask her to leave. Well, she might as well make it easy for him.

"No problem," she said. "I've already found other accommodations. I'll—"

"What are you talking about?" he interrupted. "I didn't say anything about your moving."

"But you said it wasn't working...."

"Yes, but I had another plan in mind." He took her hand. "Marry me, Zana. The arrangement needs to change because we're living not together, but side by side. We should be married. We can have a simple wedding right here at Zachary House. Then before long, children... Just think how happy it would make everyone."

Outraged, Zana stood, pulling her hand from his grasp. "You've really got this all figured out, haven't you? Marriage. Children. And just to make people happy—your mother, in particular. Well, you can find yourself another bride." Despite her fury she managed to keep her voice restrained, because she didn't want to be overheard by any household staff who might not yet have left for the night.

"Please, sit back down," he said. After she did so, he gently caressed her cheek. "At least give it some consideration. Don't turn me down before you've thought it over."

"I don't need to think it over. The idea is absurd. You don't love me. And I . . . I don't love you." She lowered her head self-consciously, focusing her eyes on the napkin she was nervously twisting around her fingers.

Brian reached out and cupped her chin, coaxing it up. "Don't you?"

She shook her head, attempting to both break contact and refute his words.

"Don't try to deny it. You know you do, and like I said before, there's passion between us."

"That's beside the point. Passion isn't enough. Anyway, what you're talking about is a marriage to placate our parents."

"Now you're being ridiculous. I said there's passion, but there's also love. You're in love with me, Zana Zachary, and I love you. Regardless of what you say."

"You don't believe in love. You once even referred to it as some sort of social disease."

"I must have been right, because it seems highly contagious."

He rose from his chair and lifted her out of hers. Before she could protest, he was kissing her, and she experienced that familiar loss of reason. But this time she fought it and pushed him away. "Please, let me go. I can't think when you do that."

He grinned. "That should tell you something—don't think."

"But one of us has to." Unable to face Brian any longer, she fled from the kitchen, ignoring his cry of, "Zana, wait!"

She ran toward the stairway with the intention of escaping to her bedroom. But as her hand clasped the banister, she realized it would be only a matter of minutes before Brian followed her there. What she needed was to get completely away from him, so she could think. Spying her handbag on the petticoat table, she grabbed it and raced out the front door.

For a moment she sat at the wheel of her car, trying to decide what to do, where to go. It was almost nine o'clock, so she didn't have many choices. She pulled out of the driveway and started driving aimlessly.

The studio? No, he'd probably follow her there, too. To Russell and Caroline's? Definitely not. The last thing she wanted was to answer questions that would arise if she showed up on their doorstep. A coffee shop wouldn't help since she couldn't stay there all night. Eventually she'd have to return to Zachary House and to Brian. And at the moment, she simply couldn't handle that.

Right now, she felt more like a little girl than a woman in love, and she longed for her mother to give her comfort and advice. But that, of course, was impossible, so she decided to settle for the next best thing—Aunt Cil. She could be in New Orleans before midnight.

Anyone but Cil would have scolded Zana for setting off so late. However, when Zana called her collect from a pay phone outside Natchez, Cil simply told her she was welcome. Zana might be agitated, but she had enough sense to realize she couldn't go pounding on her aunt's door in the middle of the night without some sort of warning.

By the time she was halfway to New Orleans, she'd become more rational and was attempting to analyze her childish decision to run away. Brian had offered marriage. That was exactly what she'd wanted, yet she'd responded as if he'd threatened her with permanent bondage.

Surely he'd expected her to fall into his arms, not disappear. Was he worried about her? She felt a twinge of guilt. Part of her acknowledged that she should have said yes. Brian was right. She *did* love him. She had for the longest time, even if she hadn't recognized the feelings she had for him as love. But was love enough? There were so many considerations.

First, her career. She was unsure of her future, but she didn't want to give up dance entirely. Would Brian expect her to?

She knew that was a small problem compared to their extended family. Brian had said he loved her, but most relationships involved only two people.

Theirs, on the other hand, also concerned Russell and Caroline. What if she and Brian broke up? How would that affect their parents' marriage?

So what to do? With relief, she found a parking spot right in front of Cil's well-lighted town house. Perhaps her aunt could provide an answer.

THEY SAT at the kitchen table drinking chamomile tea and listening to Sid's soft cat snores. Brian had called before Zana arrived; he was "worried sick," Cil said.

"I can't tell you what to do, dear. You're the only one who can make that decision. It was easy for me and Justin. We loved each other, and everyone approved of our marriage. The only sad part was that your father had already left and couldn't be at my wedding.

"But then I lost my husband. I thought I'd go mad those first few years. The pain was horrible. I can tell you one thing, though. I'd go through that suffering again if I could have just one more hour with him...." Cil was patting Zana's hands, but her eyes were distant, her thoughts obviously on her adored Justin.

"Unfortunately love doesn't come with a guarantee." Cil went to the stove to boil some more water. "But then, I guess you know that. Have you thought that might be the reason you're frightened, Zana? Has losing Vivi made you afraid to love again?"

"But I *do* love him."

"Then there's your answer." She smiled at her niece.

Zana returned the smile, the shackles of indecision suddenly falling away. Perhaps her method had been rather haphazard, but at least now she knew what to do.

The drive back to Natchez seemed a thousand miles long. Zana had to constantly watch the speedometer, each check revealing that she was driving too fast. It was now near dawn and she'd had no sleep, but that didn't matter. The important thing was getting back to Brian.

Zachary House was quiet when she unlocked the front door and went inside. She checked downstairs, but Brian was nowhere in sight. Obviously he was still in bed. Zana ran to his room and knocked on his door. Sounds from the other side told her Brian was rushing to open it. When he did, he was disheveled—unshaven, shirtless and still dressed in the jeans he'd worn the night before. But to Zana he looked wonderful.

"The answer is yes!" she said and flung herself into his arms.

"I KNEW IT, I just knew it!" Lucille gushed, as if this was the first she'd heard of the proposal. "The day the two of you arrived on my doorstep looking for Russell and Caroline, well, I knew it right then. Of course, you gave us all a fright with that living-together bit.'' She embraced Zana, then Brian, almost squeezing them breathless in her exuberance. ''It'll be the event of the season! Instead of the ball, we'll have the wedding—isn't it lucky that we haven't already ordered the invitations? A wedding. Right here at Zachary House. Just like Mama and Papa.''

Cil put Sid's carrier on the floor, then took off her hat, this one adorned with colored feathers, and placed it on a nearby chair. They were standing in the front hall where Zana and Brian had greeted Cil and their parents with the news of their engagement.

Russell hugged his daughter and shook Brian's hand, looking every bit as pleased as Lucille.

If it was possible, Caroline seemed even more pleased. ''We must celebrate. Do we have champagne?'' Her arm around Zana's waist, she steered the group toward the back of the house. ''You're exactly what Brian needs in his life. I couldn't be happier, my dear.''

The five congregated in the kitchen, sipping the bubbly wine and preparing dinner. Brian had given Maudie the afternoon off, but she'd set the dining room table before leaving and had placed foil-wrapped potatoes to bake in the oven. Brian and Russell went outside to start the patio grill and watch over beef fillets and shrimp. The women chopped vegetables for a salad and spread a loaf of French bread with garlic butter, all the while talking about the wedding.

To Zana's surprise, she wasn't uncomfortable; instead, she felt strangely invigorated. And why not? she thought, giving full rein to the orange-blossom giddiness she was experiencing. All the laughter and planning and joy was wonderful. Maybe it was old-fashioned, but she liked being in the kitchen with her aunt and stepmother, liked the way the men presided over the grill outside.

Family. That was one reason she'd had trouble making the decision to go to London. If she'd left Natchez, she'd have missed her father, missed Aunt Cil. Although she was still adjusting to Russell's marriage, Zana realized she'd have missed Caroline, too.

Now that Russell had gotten used to Brian, and Brian had accepted his mother's marriage, they'd become a family. And that was something Zana didn't want to lose.

Later, the small group was eating at the table, and Zana tried to picture them in five years. By then there might be a grandchild. Maybe two. Instinctively she rubbed her midsection. It was possible that by next fall, she could be pregnant. The thought made her flush, and she became aware of Brian sitting beside her. He reached over and took her hand. Had he been able to read her mind?

"I plan to turn that attic upside down looking for it," Cil was saying. "I think it would be *so* romantic for Zana to wear the same gown Mama did—the one we saw in their wedding picture. The Zacharys saved everything, you know. If the mice or other varmints haven't destroyed the dress, then it may be okay for Zana to wear."

"Surely it was put in a cedar trunk," Russell said.

"I simply don't remember. Being so much taller than Mama I just didn't give a thought to it when I married, then after the bankruptcy..." Her voice trailed off. That had been an unhappy time for Cil. Zana realized how much it meant to her aunt, as well as her father, to have the old estate back in the family, ready to pass on to Zachary descendants. By marrying Brian, she'd make a lot of people happy, including herself. It really was the right thing to do.

"The dress was old when Mama wore it, you know. It was *her* mother's." Cil once again sounded cheerful; she never let herself stay sad for long. "We can search for it, but it might be better to find a dressmaker who can make a copy—if that's what Zana wants." She glanced at her niece.

"I think that's a wonderful idea," Zana said, allowing herself to be swept up in Cil's excitement. Besides, she couldn't help but be pleased that three people very dear to her unconditionally approved of her marriage.

But what was Brian feeling? He certainly *seemed* happy. His hand was still holding hers and now his thumb was stroking her palm. Zana wasn't sure whether his mind was on the wedding or, more likely, the wedding night.

"So what do you two have to say?" Cil asked. Then as she watched them exchange smiles, she tittered, "Quit making cow eyes at each other. You'll have plenty of time for that later. Right now we need to come to a decision about the date. If we wait until October, it'll conflict with Fall Pilgrimage. How about late September? The garden will still be in flower then, and the roses will probably start blooming again after the heat of summer has passed. We can set up an altar on the patio. We can invite—"

"Whoa," Brian interrupted, his voice good-natured, but firm. "Everything sounds fine to me. It's really up to Zana, though, but how about keeping it small? We don't know a lot of people in Natchez, anyway. Right?" He looked at Zana for confirmation and, after she nodded, continued, "I'll want to have my staff. It's not a big group, but we're close. Most of them will have relocated by then, and it's only a short drive for the others. Then, of course, family and whoever else Zana includes, but not too many."

Zana appreciated his restraining her aunt. There would be enough to do before a small wedding, and she didn't want to have to deal with a three-ring circus. If Cil had her way she'd invite half the city.

Lucille still had a lot of friends here, people she'd known all her life. But they were no longer close to Russell, who'd shunned any kind of social activity on his return to the city. Later, he'd been too involved with Caroline to make new friends or get reacquainted with old ones.

And the people of Natchez were mostly strangers to Zana. She knew Jeff and his staff, was acquainted with a few people who worked near her studio, the women in her aerobics classes, the mothers of her younger students and a couple of others, but that was all, and she didn't really feel close to any of them. She was happy to let Cil and Caroline have fun with the wedding; but she didn't want to share her special day with a houseful of strangers.

When the meal was over, everyone helped clear the table, then took a stroll in the garden. Eventually Russell checked his watch. "It's getting late."

"So romantic, so romantic," Cil said with an appreciative sigh, as she hugged and kissed Zana and Brian, then left with Caroline and Russell.

Zana watched the taillights of the car until they were out of sight. "They probably think we're upstairs in bed by now."

"What a great idea." Brian wrapped an arm around her shoulder.

"No, I don't think so."

"Most prospective bridegrooms at least get a good-night kiss."

"I recall a couple of kisses that were almost my undoing. Let's save our... Let's wait until..." She didn't continue, unsure what Brian was going to say.

His expression was thoughtful. Eventually he spoke. "Until the wedding night? Okay, if that's what you want. But I warn you that I won't have an easy time waiting. I've never been a patient man, as you well know." He smiled, and Zana lowered her head, hiding the flush she could feel in her cheeks.

"Dammit! I want to kiss you, I want to feel your lips on mine, your body against mine." He moved closer until she could feel the warmth of his breath on her face. He cradled her jaw in his hand, and tilted her head toward his, allowing their mouths to meet. Gently he kissed her, but soon they both wanted more. Zana's arms were around his neck while his hands stroked her body.

"Have there been others, Zana?" He broke the kiss, and she nestled her head against his shoulder.

Startled by the question, she couldn't form a response. Besides, she didn't want to reveal too much. He was experienced; she was not. She might have seen a lot of the world, but she wasn't worldly. Her obsession with dancing had taken most of her time and energy. Before Brian, she'd resisted all attempted seductions. She didn't know whether that was because she'd been too involved in ballet, or because Brian was the first man she'd ever loved.

"Don't answer that question," he said. "I had no right to ask it, and I think I know the response, anyway." He stepped back, putting some space between them. "I'm not sure why I'm the guy who won your heart, but I'll tell you why I'm marrying you. I love you and I've longed to make love to you since the day we met. I want to run my fingers through your hair." With those words, he untied the ribbon holding her braid, sending a cascade of black waves down her back. Gently he smoothed the hair he'd released.

He gave her a tender smile. "Still, the idea of a wedding night with a bride who's never been with a man is surprisingly appealing. Impatient as I am, I think I can manage to hold on. But we'd better tell Mother and Lucille to get on with the plans—I can't wait too long."

BRIAN SPENT MOST of the next month in Memphis, completing his company's move to Natchez. He called Zana every evening and came home at least one night a weekend. And to show her he was thinking of her, he sent flowers—sometimes roses, other times colorful bouquets of carnations, zinnias, and irises.

Six months earlier, Zana would never have imagined she'd be this happy. It was almost as if she'd found her destiny. All her life when she'd listened to her father's stories about his home, she'd felt as if Natchez and Zachary House were part of her, too. Her mother often told her there was a plan for everyone. Had this been the plan for her?

Zana smiled to herself. Her life could almost be a ballet story. She recalled how she'd always managed to dance with intense emotion, a feat she achieved not by drawing on personal experience, but attributable strictly to her talent. She'd never been able to understand the desire, the joy created by one's love for another person—until now. She thought of Brian.

Even providence seemed to support her marriage to him. The day after they'd announced their engagement, Zana had been invited by the board of directors for the International Ballet Competitions to become one of its Mississippi members and be on the planning committee for the next session in Jackson. She'd also attend future competitions outside the United States.

Zana experienced a surge of excitement at the prospect of visiting Varna, Helsinki and Moscow again. It was a wonderful opportunity for her to stay involved in the work she adored—perhaps the next best thing to dancing.

Brian voiced no objections to having a traveling wife—he even expressed a wish to join her occasionally. He encouraged her to keep her studio in Natchez, too, if she wanted. She was pleased he felt that way because she had no intention of abandoning the studio now. Although the competitions gave her a challenge that was currently missing from her career, she genuinely liked teaching.

The only moment of distress came when she called Kurt to tell him she wouldn't be accepting the position. But, as they talked, it became obvious that Kurt had been creating a place for her, that in reality there was no opening.

Zana was relieved her life once again had purpose, and she was glad to be a part of international ballet, although it meant getting used to the absence of applause. However, she was trading hard work and sacrifice and the roar of the crowd for an opportunity to inspire young dancers and marriage to Brian. Not a difficult choice. Zana smiled again. Not a difficult choice at all.

THE TIME BEFORE the wedding passed quickly. Soon it was an afternoon in late September, and Zana was standing in her bedroom at Zachary House in front of a full-length mirror. Through the open draperies she had a clear view of storm clouds gathering overhead and faraway flashes of lightning.

Zana had never been superstitious, but the gloomy skies concerned her. All week Aunt Cil had been nattering about how "happy is the bride the sun shines on," and the sun hadn't made an appearance since yesterday. Zana hoped this wasn't a bad omen.

Her fretting was interrupted by a gentle tap on the door, then Aunt Cil came into the room followed by Sid—who wore a bow tie instead of a collar. "Need some help?" Cil asked.

"I'm ready to slip into the gown, and I'd appreciate another pair of hands." Just then a gust of wind sent tree limbs scraping across the window.

"Dear me," Zana sighed, gesturing with her head toward the heaving branches. "What do you have to say about the sun shining on the bride today?"

If she thought this turn of the weather would daunt her aunt, Zana was underestimating Lucille. "Oh, that," Cil replied, as though it was only a trifle that a hundred folding chairs had to be transferred from the garden to the salon, along with tables, the altar, the flowers and two candelabras. Even the food pavilion had been dismantled, and the buffet set up in the ballroom.

"Not to worry," Cil added. "It's just history repeating itself. It rained the day Mama and Papa married, too. And they had a wonderful twenty years together before she passed away. Papa might have been rather dictatorial, but he adored Mama. He kept that portrait of her in the bedroom till the day he died—the first thing he saw in the morning, the last thing at night."

With a laugh, Cil sighed. "Sometimes I wish I could find that kind of devotion again. A man to love... Oh, dear, don't mind me. Weddings always make me sentimental." Lucille eased the wedding dress from its hanger and held it out for Zana.

Zana was touched by her aunt's words and, as she stepped into the dress, wondered what could be done for Cil. Zana smiled—perhaps matchmaking was contagious. She realized that she could start with a well-aimed toss of her bouquet, then she'd see if Brian knew any suitable bachelors. With that decided, she looked at herself in the mirror.

Her dress was a replica of her grandmother's gown, expertly made by a local seamstress. Zana's raven hair was pinned back from her face and set in a chignon of curls interspersed with lace ribbons. She wore no veil and her only jewelry, other than her engagement ring, was a strand of pearls with matching earrings, a gift from Brian delivered just that morning.

Lucille stepped back to gaze at her niece. "Oh my. Oh my... it's like I'm seeing Mama in her youth." She pulled a handkerchief from the bosom of her violet crepe shift and dabbed at her eyes, futilely trying to prevent a streak of black mascara from staining her cheek. She rustled through her large purse for her makeup case, did some repairs, then adjusted her new hat, a violet turban-style creation she'd had made to match her dress. For Cil, it was an understated outfit. "Now where's that brother of mine?" she asked impatiently as the clock in the hallway chimed two.

Since Zana knew so few people in Natchez, she'd asked six ten-year-olds from her ballet classes to be her attendants. In Europe, children often accompanied the bride and, despite her Natchez roots, Zana was more European than American. Like Zana, the children wore white, but the sashes of their dresses were in bright pastels.

Russell stuck his head in the door. "It's time," he said with a smile. As he opened the door farther, a sonata by a string quartet could be heard. Cil kissed her niece and headed next door to hustle the little bridesmaids toward the stairs.

Walking down the aisle, Zana focused on the altar. Brian was waiting there, and she knew without a doubt that this was the only man she'd ever love.

The music, the ceremony, everything was flawless—except for the continued rumblings from the threatening sky.

As the couple repeated their vows, a jagged bolt of lightning, then a clap of thunder stopped Zana in midsentence. She waited a few moments before resuming. The rest of the ceremony concluded without any further interruptions from the elements, and soon Brian was pulling her into his arms and murmuring in her ear.

"I love you, and I'm becoming absolutely intrigued with thunderstorms. The nicest things happen to me when it's raining—I met you, I married you. I only hope the downpour continues all night."

His lips touched hers in a brief kiss of promise, a promise of passion to come. As they turned to accept the congratulations of their family and friends, Zana felt wonderful, because she knew they'd married for all the right reasons. The only reason—love.

Fifty red-blooded, white-hot, true-blue hunks from every State in the Union!

Beginning in May, look for MEN MADE IN AMERICA! Written by some of our most popular authors, these stories feature fifty of the strongest, sexiest men, each from a different state in the union!

Two titles available every other month at your favorite retail outlet.

In September, look for:

DECEPTIONS by Annette Broadrick (California)
STORMWALKER by Dallas Schulze (Colorado)

In November, look for:

STRAIGHT FROM THE HEART by Barbara Delinsky (Connecticut)
AUTHOR'S CHOICE by Elizabeth August (Delaware)

You won't be able to resist MEN MADE IN AMERICA!

Calloway Corners

In September, Harlequin is proud to bring readers four involving, romantic stories about the Calloway sisters, set in Calloway Corners, Louisiana. Written by four of Harlequin's most popular and award-winning authors, you'll be enchanted by these sisters and the men they love!

MARIAH by Sandra Canfield
JO by Tracy Hughes
TESS by Katherine Burton
EDEN by Penny Richards

As an added bonus, you can enter a sweepstakes contest to win a trip to Calloway Corners, and meet all four authors. Watch for details in all Calloway Corners books in September.

**HARLEQUIN CELEBRATES
THE SEASON OF SHARING
AND FAMILY WITH**

Friends, Families, Lovers

Harlequin introduces the latest member in its family of
seasonal collections. Following in the footsteps of the popular
My Valentine, Just Married and *Harlequin Historical Christmas
Stories,* we are proud to present FRIENDS, FAMILIES,
LOVERS. A collection of three new contemporary romance
stories about America at its best, about welcoming others into
the circle of love.... Stories to warm your heart...

By three leading romance authors:

**KATHLEEN EAGLE
SANDRA KITT
RUTH JEAN DALE**

Available in October, wherever
Harlequin books are sold.